Río de Dios

Río de Dios

Thirteen Histories of the Los Angeles River

Bruce Bartrug, Peter Bowler
& Charles Hood

RED HEN PRESS | Los Angeles, California

Río de Dios: Thirteen Histories of the Los Angeles River

Book design by Mark E. Cull & Richard Niño.

Back cover photograph, *Model shows proposed improvements*,
Herald Examiner Collection/Los Angeles Public Library.
Front cover photograph, *Dominguez Channel*, by Charles Hood.
Photograph on page 144, *Confluence 2*, by Charles Hood.

ISBN: 978-1-59709-090-2
Library of Congress Catalog Card Number: 2007931674

The City of Los Angeles Department of Cultural Affairs, Los Angeles County Arts Commission and National Endowment for the Arts partially support Red Hen Press.

Published by Red Hen Press
www.redhen.org

First Edition

Acknowledgments

Bruce Bartrug: First, a gentle and endless *thank you* to my wife, Michele, who has the patience of a saint. Thanks also to Angela Percival, a salmon ecologist and fellow artist, for the detailed information about the western brook lamprey. Thank you to Louis Agassiz Fuertes (1874-1927) for reminding us about the difference between one's best work and that which is merely good, even if many of us do not have the time to put that distinction into practice. A bow as well to my list-serve friends in the Guild of Natural History Illustrators. And lastly, thanks to Charles Hood and Red Hen Press for yet another opportunity to test my wife's patience.

Peter Bowler: I gratefully thank Camm Swift for courteously providing me with the best information available about the fish fauna of the Los Angeles River. I am indebted to Kimball Garrett for his excellent contributions to what we know about the ecology of the river and greatly appreciate his review of the manuscript. Bill Bretz and Phil Pister are inspirational to my interest in wetland restoration and are examples themselves of how effective individuals can be in protecting and raising the ecological condition of damaged wetlands. The resiliency and perseverance of life in even the most dire of ecological degradation amazes me, and the promise of fostering its restoration to any degree was encouraging as I worked on this book. I thank the Friends of the Los Angeles

River for their courageous and constructive defense of the L.A. River, and I thank FoLAR for its critical role in stimulating the creation of the revitalization plans now in place. Allan Schoenherr read and was encouraging about an early draft of the manuscript. My wife Crissy supported me wholeheartedly throughout the entire process of researching and developing this manuscript. Charles Hood is a friend and poet whose scholarship, insight, originality, and skill immediately attracted me to work with him on this project—and I am pleased to be a part of his immersion in his home waters.

CHARLES HOOD: I want to thank the Center for Land Use Interpretation—always the belle of the ball, whether one is studying parking lots, abandoned quarries, or the ice runways of Antarctica—as well as the Huntington Library in San Marino, the Research Library at the Getty Center, the Academic Senate Grant and Staff Development Committees of Antelope Valley College, the staff in the science libraries of UCLA, UC Riverside, UC Irvine, and UC Santa Barbara, and, lastly, the crews at Los Angeles Helicopters, based out of Long Beach Airport. Any folks who say "Sure, no problem," when asked to take the doors off their helicopters are all right by me.

Want to help or find out more? Please contact FoLAR, the Friends of the Los Angeles River, via their website or at 570 W. Ave. 26, Suite 250, Los Angeles, CA 90065.

Merced de Papel asked me where my father and I were going. I told her that we were going to Los Angeles so he could work in a dress factory and I could go to school and learn about a world built on cement. Merced de Papel was going to Los Angeles too, but for different reasons. She had heard that Los Angeles was the last refuge for those who had lost their civilization and were afraid of the rain.

—*The People of Paper*,
Salvador Plascencia

Contents

The First History

Monday's Madonna: The L.A. River and the Hopeful Science of Restoration Ecology

by Peter Bowler

The Second History

Water from Stone

by Bruce Bartrug

Histories Three to Thirteen

Harder Than Light

by Charles Hood

for Ben Saltman,

friend and mentor

Monday's Madonna

The L.A. River and the

Hopeful Science of Restoration Ecology

by Peter Bowler

And so castles made of sand slip into the sea, eventually

—Jimi Hendrix

Ask not, what good is an endangered species;

ask, what good are you?

—Phil Pister

Numbers (and Other Facts)

The Los Angeles River is a multi-tributary hydraulic arterial system that embraces a watershed of 2,155 square kilometers and whose drainage resembles a deflating balloon or a strange stomach with a narrowing channel as it approaches the ocean. From its origin at the confluence of Bell Creek and Calabasas Wash in the San Fernando Valley, it descends its gradient and historic floodplain 82 kilometers (51 miles) to its union with the Pacific Ocean in the Long Beach harbor. Historically, most of its water was derived from the surrounding San Gabriel and Santa Susana Mountains. Today the water flows from the Owens Valley through the septis of Los Angeles and exits the Tillman Reclamation Plant, reemerging as the modern river. From upstream to down, larger tributaries include Brown's Canyon Wash, Aliso Canyon Wash, Tujunga Wash, Western Burbank Channel, Verdugo Wash, Arroyo Seco, Rio Hondo, and Compton Creek. In a state with 1,400 dams, these days it has the dubious reputation among Western river systems as being the most straightened, channelized, and hardscaped of them all. Snout to vent data reveal that in its length of roughly 378 kilometers of bed plus tributaries, a meager 12% of its reaches are in natural condition. Taken as a whole, well over half the river isn't a river at all—it's a wet streak through a flood control basin. As Faber (1989) sardonically notes, "For its size, the Los Angeles River may be the most extensively controlled river in the world. There are 290 check dams, 75 debris dams, eight control and storage reservoirs, and two large flood-control basins in its drainage basin." Since dams are sediment and nutrient traps, the river's chakras are blocked 375 times by impounding structures alone, and natural sediment and nutrient flow through the gradient is completely impeded. The habitat losses in the Los Angeles River basin mirror and contribute to the state's estimated 91% loss of wetland habitat and the 97% loss of floodplain riparian habitat in Southern California. As C.S. Lewis's marshwiggles would say, "What rum little creatures humans are." Commensal we are not.

Water (and Other Fictions)

With a cumulative score of 0.9 GPA, the Los Angeles River consistently gets a resounding F from the Friends of the L.A. River (FoLAR) in water quality monitoring at 22 sites. A few sites averaged a C, such as Arroyo Seco, but most gauge stations from Owensmouth to Wardlow Road spike straight F's in test after test. During the dry season, in its Mediterranean climate, most of its water is reclaimed—meaning the mother liquor of treated human sewage spread over an anthropocentric landscape. Before the re-use of treated human sewage for the irrigation of exotic landscapes, the lower reaches of the river were actually dry during the summer in drought years, but today a foamy urban slobber drools down the trough year-round.

Some of that slick green slaver accumulates via the 2,200 storm drains that empty into the river corridor throughout its course. Most commentary uses the metaphor of a corset, inspired perhaps by the fact that there are 110 road crossings lacing its descent to the ocean. Legal jurisdiction cinches it wincingly tight as well, given that there are over two dozen competing communities through which it shuffles its way. Yet who is responsible for what remains unclear, ten million pages of litigation later. Who is in charge of making sure that stray dogs don't chase off desperately weary sandpipers, feeding in Long Beach after migrating from tundra breeding grounds? Who will clean up the plastic bottles, or lobby the Feds for better anadromous fish management? Aging oil pipelines crisscross Los Angeles just under the surface, as Bill Fox notes in his L.A. meditation, *Making Time*. Rusting and gurgling, they remain hazards undiagnosed and uninspected. Yet potential disaster waits close at hand. As he reminds us, in "Long Beach in 1994, for instance, twenty-four thousand barrels of petroleum-contaminated water leaked into the Los Angeles River, necessitating the replacement of more than twenty miles of pipe." Other spills "have drained out into, and helped pollute" the river's mouth and other coastal waters. All in all, much of the modern river is a kind of existential nightmare for river ecologists—a thin, often frothy meniscus bleeding and oozing its way down a concrete trough.

At the mouth, soft-bottom (areas not armored with concrete, but having soil as a substrate) extends from the Willow Street Bridge to Queensway Bay. This 2.6-mile reach is fully tidal from the mouth upstream to Willow Street, with benthic salinities at the mouth of 33 parts per thousand in the fall to 26.4 ppt in the winter. The more dense seawater slides beneath the fresh in a salt wedge, with surface salinities at the mouth being between 29 ppt in the fall and 24.3 in the winter.

Hard to conceive how different this was not so long ago. The fabric and detail of the historic floodplain is now lost, but the California Coastal Conservancy has stated that it generally consisted of "extensive marshes, streams, lakes, and seeps covering much of present day downtown Los Angeles to San Pedro Bay and eastward to the San Gabriel River." It was one of the largest floodplains on the California coast, with a watershed of 834 square miles, and its final transformation into a flood control conduit was completed in 1954. A glimpse of what it may have been like can be found in the journals of Aldo Leopold, when he camped in the delta of the Colorado River in the 1930s. "The still waters," he wrote, "were of a deep emerald hue, colored by algae, I suppose, but no less green for all that. A verdant wall of mesquite and willow separated the channel from the thorny desert beyond. At each bend we saw egrets standing in the pools ahead, each white statue matched by its white reflection. Fleets of cormorants drove their black prows in quest of skittering mullets; avocets, willets, and yellowlegs dozed one-legged on the bars; mallards, widgeons, and teal sprang skyward in alarm. As the birds took to the air, they accumulated in a small cloud ahead, there to settle, or to break back to our rear. When a troop of egrets settled on a far green willow, they looked like a premature snowstorm." This evocative description comes from "Green Lagoons," a chapter in his greatest legacy, *Sand County Almanac*, a book with as much to offer Los Angeles now as ever before.

Science confirms the keenings of poets and canoe-paddle philosophers. After all, the effects of channelization are now well known and include the many maladies of this stream of poor karma (see Tables 1 and 3). Among the problems with straightened and hardscaped channels are a very substantive increase in water temperatures when compared with a natural stream due to a lack of shading from riparian vegetation, and this in turn ties in with a lack of cover for fish. This causes rapid and severe daily and seasonal fluctuations in temperatures, and means as well that there is no input of leaf litter, which is the basis of the energy and food base for natural streams. Worse, habitat surrogates like these are primarily riffle with unsorted gravel, if any, as a substrate, and during runoff events, water moves faster than most aquatic organisms can withstand, so they are swept away since there is no heterogeneity in the bottom environment and hence no place for organisms to rest or hide (based upon Faber, 1989).

A side note on the ferocity of such swift water may be in order, since it is no small thing to take away all the crannies fish need to be able to survive the rare but intense winter rainstorms. (Members of urban swiftwater rescue teams may find this of particular interest.) Leveling a river and taking away the rocks and brush and hidey-holes is sort of like asking a person to survive a Category IV hurricane by walking naked along a breakwater while holding aloft a cardboard sail, rather than being given a slicker, a flashlight, and a very thick concrete wall to hunker behind. It just can't be done—at least not for long. A river in flood presents fluid dynamics in "near-infinite complexity," as David Quammen has explored in an essay titled "Vortex." If you "follow the subject of fluid dynamics into its technical literature," then you quickly come to "concepts such as turbulence, laminar flow, viscosity, Reynolds number, boundary layer, shear stress, Bénard cells, and vorticity." It gets worse. "Within another page or three you're bound to encounter some nosebleed-inducing mathematics." What it all adds up to is a very muddy, very fast, very fierce jet stream of water, the kind of churning deluge that uproots trees and smashes retaining walls like a battering ram, and once you do that to a river, native aquatic life becomes seriously degraded. That is because the natural alteration of pools and riffles in a meandering stream with point bars and cut banks is absent, and very few native species can endure these kinds of artificial, straightened, canalized conditions. Making one kind of change changes everything else.

Last, a fluvial system would normally include an erosion zone at the headwaters where sediment is eroded and flows in the system, a zone of storage and transport of sediment in the middle (and usually flatter) section of the stream, and a zone of deposition of sediment—in the case of the Los Angeles River, this would have been the ocean and the beaches thereof. Needless to say, since sediment is captured in the basins of the middle zone, this passage of sediment materials through the system has been stopped, leaving the river bed wet but dead. The classic result of blocking sediment flow through rivers is an armored bottom, with little sand or gravel—merely a swept bed of lifeless rock (or concrete, as the case may be).

Table 1. Differences between a channelized and a natural stream (adapted from Faber, 1989):

NATURAL STREAM CHARACTERISTICS:	ARTIFICIAL CHANNEL (CHANNELIZED STREAM):
• Surface water temperatures are suitable to sustain native species. • There is adequate shading because of the presence of riparian vegetation. • Good cover for fish life. • Shading plus a pool and riffle sequence mean minimal variation in temperatures. • There is abundant leaf material input. • Sorted gravels provide diversified habitats for many stream organisms.	• Increased water temperatures. • No shading or riparian habitat. • No cover for fish life. • Rapid daily and seasonal fluctuations in water temperatures. • Reduced or no leaf material input. • Very little algae and few macrophytes.
Pool environment during high flow: • There is a diversity of water velocities: low in pools, higher in riffles. • Resting areas are abundant beneath undercut banks or behind large rocks, and so forth.	Pool environment during high flow: • May have stream velocity higher than most aquatic life can withstand. • Few or no resting places.
Pool environment during low flow: • In pool environments during low flow there is sufficient water depth to support fish and other aquatic life during the dry season.	Pool environment during low flow: • Insufficient depth of flow during dry seasons to support diversity of fish and aquatic life. Few if any pools (all riffle).

Channelized stream segments are homogeneous habitats, support little species diversity, and sustain a meager representation of the native fauna. Hardscaping (concrete and non-permeable surfaces) causes much greater floods with higher flows than occur in natural wetlands where natural floodplain processes occur. Natural wetlands absorb flooding by swelling as water is stored in underground aquifers, then releasing it slowly.

Lost Links and Empty Aquifers

The connectedness derived from Vannote's river continuum concept, linking the flow headwater to estuary, is shattered here, replaced instead by a homogeneous and prosthetic artifice that is hostile to most life, rather than the stratigraphic ballet of sorted aquatic insect and fish groups as one descends a natural stream. In a pristine stream system, the headwaters are characterized by dense overshading riparian vegetation that sheds leaves and organic debris (coarse particulate organic matter, or CPOM) into the nutrient-poor (oligotrophic), clear headwaters. This organic material can form as much as 90% of the energy moving through a lotic (flowing) system, and the headwater reaches are dominated by aquatic insects whose mouth parts are specialized to shred leaves ("shredders"), as well as some predators and collectors that filter small, fine particulate organic matter (FPOM) from the water column. The middle section of the stream is wider, has some nutrients in the water, and sunlight can penetrate the water column to the bottom, stimulating algal and aquatic weed growth. In this middle reach area of the stream, a group of scraping and grazing specialists ("grazers") scour the benthic (bottom) environment, eating algal films and plants, and there is a strong presence of collectors harvesting the FPOM drifting downstream from the headwaters. In the lowest reaches of the idealized river, there is nothing to graze upon because the murkiness of the water prevents sunlight from penetrating to the bottom, and there is no CPOM, thus collectors dominate. Predators are a minor component of each of the three stream sections. Table 2 summarizes these points (pp. 26–27).

This description shows how it should be—and for thousands of years, how it was. Now it's different of course. Despite tiny fragments of a healthy headwater setting, the middle and lowest reaches of the Los Angeles River have been sacrificed. As Jenny Price recently noted, "The cement channel . . . constitutes L.A.'s strategy to move storm water, that life-giving natural resource, through the city. A city with a semi-arid Mediterranean climate pours as much rainwater (which we get from the sky for free) as possible into the storm sewers, through the river, and into the Pacific—and then pays dearly to import water by aqueduct from up to 400 miles away. Call it watering the ocean, by draining watersheds across the West" (Price, 2007).

The U.S. Army Corps of Engineers and the Los Angeles County Department of Public Works, who periodically clear sediment and the struggling vegetation to maintain flood control capacity, operate the channelized river course itself. The riverbed is principally sand with surficial silts. The river's water quality is highly impaired, and does not meet existing standards for pH, AMM, lead, coliform, trash, scum algae, total dissolved solids, and turbidity.

It's hard to know what to do with realities such as these. Just because we have heard it before does not make it any less true. What response is appropriate? How does one sort out these facts? Writing as a father, teacher, ecologist, and lover of the natural world, I often search for metaphors to explain basic ideas such as these, following the theory that an image is worth a thousand smolts. To illustrate the impoverishment of hard-bottom channels to my freshwater biology classes, I use slides of the channelized Los Angeles River and present it as a sort of open tomb exhibit—a grave from which the native species have long been raptured. Seeing the pictures, it is starkly obvious that it didn't have to be this way, and that nature (and natural wisdom) has come in pretty close to last place.

Table 2. Characteristics of headwater, mid-reach, and large river settings. (adapted from Vannote, 1980, and Bowler, 1988):

Characteristics of Natural Headwater Stream Segments:
• Stream Order 1-3 (0.5 - 6 meters)—small, narrow stream
• dense riparian vegetation
• closed canopy—shady, light limited
• cold, constant water temperature (spring-like; oligotrophic); clear
• gravel bottom; erosion zone of the stream
• heavy litter load and abundant coarse particulate organic matter (CPOM)
• high gradient, usually with steep valley sides; sediment shedding area of the stream
• mostly riffle habitat; high in elevation (rapid drop in elevation)
• low aquatic primary productivity—secondary producers feed on CPOM
• Productivity/Respiration ratio (P/R<1) is less than 1; very little algae or macrophytes; shredders feed on leaves
• CPOM is converted to FPOM; collectors eat FPOM directly
• predators include trout, sculpins, stoneflies, and others
• heterotrophic community
• 100-250 species of invertebrates

Table 2 (*continued*)

CONDITIONS IN THE MID-REACH OF THE RIVER:

- Stream Order 3-6 (4-75 meters)
- shift from a heterotrophic to an autotrophic community due to widening of the river, with less shading by riparian vegetation, more light penetration, thus more primary productivity
- warmer water
- producers are algae (periphyton) and attached macrophytes are present (weedy patches of plants in the stream)
- not shaded or light-limited
- shallow and clear water
- suckers, some trout, bottom and grazing fish
- area of sediment transport; some sediment on the bottom
- high nutrient levels derived from upstream
- because there is an increasing quantity of FPOM, collectors are abundant, shredders decrease because there is nothing to shred (no leaves); grazers are abundant, feeding on periphyton
- invertebrate and vertebrate predators present
- autotrophic community-ratio of photosynthesis to respiration greater than 1 ($P/R>1$)
- 200-500 species of invertebrates

LOWERMOST SECTIONS—NOT PRESENT IN THE MODERN L.A. RIVER SYSTEM:

- Stream Orders 6-12 (up to 700 meters)
- collector species dominate because of large amounts of FPOM
- primary producers are phytoplankton, and productivity is low—FPOM and Dissolved Organic Matter (DOM) are abundant, drifting down from upstream
- the water is turbid (murky), there is low light penetration; a soft, silty/sandy bottom; homogeneous habitat
- heterotrophic community because of reduced primary productivity through increased turbidity and unstable substrates
- little species diversity among the benthic collectors; collectors filtering the water column dominate; no shredders or grazers present
- predators are aquatic beetles and bottom feeding fishes
- the photosynthesis to respiration is less than 1 due to FPOM input from upstream and despite weak primary production by phytoplankton, not periphyton ($P/R<1$)
- 50-75 species of invertebrates

Table 3. Differences between channelized and natural streams (drawn by Bruce Bartrug; adapted from Faber, 1989).

NATURAL CHANNEL	ARTIFICIAL CHANNEL
ENVIRONMENTAL CONDITIONS:  Suitable water temperatures; adequate shading; good cover for fish life; minimal variation in temperatures; abundant leaf material input.	ENVIRONMENTAL CONDITIONS:  Increased water temperatures; no shading; no cover for fish life; rapid daily and seasonal temperature fluctuations; reduced leaf material input.
POOL-RIFFLE SEQUENCE:  Sorted gravel provide diversified habitats for many stream organisms.	POOL-RIFFLE SEQUENCE:  Unsorted gravels result in a reduction in habitats and few organisms.
POOL ENVIRONMENT: HIGH FLOW 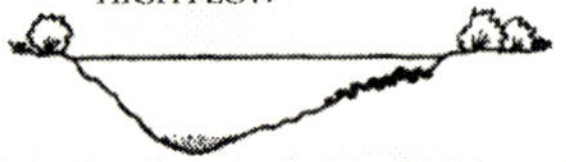 Diversity of water velocities; high in pools, lower in riffles. Abundant resting areas beneath undercut banks, behind large rocks, etc. LOW FLOW  Sufficient water depth to support fish and other aquatic life during dry season.	POOL ENVIRONMENT: HIGH FLOW  May have stream velocity higher than some aquatic life can withstand. Few or no resting places. LOW FLOW  Insufficient depth of flow during dry seasons to support diversity of fish and aquatic life. Few if any pools (all riffles).

Backing Up

But this situation is only a paused video frame of the landscape of modern times. Let us respool the tape slightly. Once, there were at least 45 Gabrielino settlements on its banks, and the river flowed to the sea unimpeded by weirs, groins, bunds, or riprap. As a general rule, the pre-Anglo habitat of Los Angeles was nearly paradisiacal, or at least seems so in smoggy hindsight. Here is Blake Gumprecht:

> Three centuries ago, the river meandered this way and that through a dense forest of willow and sycamore, elderberry, and wild grape. Its overflow filled vast marshlands that were home to myriad waterfowl and small animals. Steelhead trout spawned in the river, and grizzly bear roamed its shores.

We might mention here the blazing orange carpets of wild poppies so vivid and expansive that they could be seen from passing schooners, geese and ducks and cranes swirling up in the tens of thousands, or, along the beaches themselves, the early Spanish reports of dead whales being feasted on, side by side, by condors and grizzlies.

It sounds like a Descanso Gardens version of the Serengeti, but as with so many things, it turns out that the relationship between First Nation inhabitants and the California landscape was more complicated (and less Edenic) than casual surveys represent. Romanticizing the past is as fallacious as demonizing it, and earlier portrayals were far too simplistic. For one thing, there was a political and cultural sophistication which contradicts the 1950s textbook notion of the Chumash and related tribes as being made up of placid, almost imbecilic children of nature. Yet there was an ecological reality as well which initial anthropologists may have undervalued. Droughts came; game died out or was overhunted; competition intensified as food resources were overexploited. Nature is never static, never utterly benign. Los Angeles was not Malibu Barbie and never had been.

Studying the data more closely reveals that before the padres began rounding up the *naturales* into adobe-walled internment camps, there still were frequent and inevitable population stresses and declines. Collected in Deverell and Hise's *Land of Sunshine*, a long, subtle essay by Mark Raab synthesizes research from many fields to problematize the notion of Early California as an unaltered ecological paradise. Even acorns, those prize fruits of trailside lecture and Living History displays, may only have been turned to in the past thousand years or so, after other, more desirable foods were eliminated or made scarce. (Basically, it is more efficient to kill something the size of a deer than to scrabble about on all fours under an oak, gathering toxic, thimble-sized nuts that have to be ground, leached, sifted, and roasted.) Yet even if the California Indians did not live in some kind of chaparral version of a 24-hour Home Town Buffet, they did, however, have access to marshes and oxbows, copses and prairies in ways which we now look back on in stupefied wonder. Their world was not perfect, but their river nearly was. Before the indigenous peoples, the ecosystem existed on its own without the help of, tolerance by, or co-existence with the human species.

Yet a positive element of modernity is that, upon reflection, we can try to remediate the sins of our cultural fathers, and attempt restoration of some kind or scope. "In dreams begin responsibilities" said Delmore Schwartz quoting Yeats, who in turn was quoting the Romantics. Parallel with but ultimately not a successful competitor to *Chinatown* water politics were alternate dreams, dreams originating in the visions of John Wesley Powell and Frederick Church, not the Board of Realtors. To pick the most significant example, Frederick Law Olmstead and Harlan Bartholomew presented a design for a linked park system tracing the L.A. River corridor in 1930, but it was not embraced by the cities. Instead, following the 1934 and 1938 floods (and despite financial shortages during the Depression), channelization, straightening, and paving increased significantly. The Olmstead and Bartholomew plan emphasized floodplain function, but the flood control structural approach (aka ditching and paving) opened valuable floodplain real estate to development and allowed building up to the river's edge. The Olmstead plan could have worked; its rejection is the City's loss.

At the same time we cannot underestimate the threat the river posed and poses. There are many dramatic photographs of the damage from the 1938 flood, which caused the loss of 119 lives. This is a problem in Southern California in part because "severe chaparral floods are quite sudden and unpredictable, not gradual" (Quinn and Keeley, 2006). They note that in "April 1926 a world record was set in the San Gabriel Mountains . . . when almost an inch of rain fell in one minute." (We pause now to imagine what that would sound like on a tin roof or beating your parka hood to shreds.) These local drenchings "are akin to the flashfloods of the Southwestern deserts, which turn previously bone dry washes and river beds into a sea of raging torrents that sweeps away all in its path. The imminent arrival of these muddy floods in the chaparral is sometimes announced by a roaring sound, with the volume and quality of an approaching fast freight train. And there is no more time to escape than to move off the railroad tracks" (Quinn and Keeley, 2006).

Staying with the iron horse image for a moment, in Mike Davis's *Ecology of Fear* there is a compelling image of a collapsing railroad bridge resulting from the river's 1938 flood (Davis, 1998, pages 17 and 70), and another of a rowboat traversing Echo Park. This flood was minor compared with one in 1861-62, when the floodplain was a vast lake covering much of the coastal area of Los Angeles and a good portion of Orange County. According to Davis, one could have rowed from the Civic Center to Newport Beach along the alignment of what is now the Interstate 5. Los Angeles is a desert, but at times a powerfully wet one.

Grocery Lists and Suckermouths

It is becoming clear by now that the channelization and hardscaping of the river transmogrified it into an aquatic freeway—a cement-lined ditch that stretches like a half-hose, replacing the historic river riparian corridor. Inventories confirm this. From antelope to *Zigadamus* lilies (also called death camas), most native species could not survive. Just to note a few of the less conspicuous absences, a series of snail species plus the clam *Anodonta* (the

California floater) vanished. So too did half of the native fish fauna, replaced by more ecologically tolerant exotics. What has been lost? The California floater could live to be 100 years old and also was used by Native Americans as a food, tool, and decoration. But briefly in its development cycle it harmlessly attaches to the fins of native fish before returning to the sand to live out its life. If there are no fish, the clams cannot survive, and according to Camm Swift, "The only native species still in the Los Angeles River drainage are the Santa Ana sucker (*Catostomus santaanae*), Santa Ana speckled dace (*Rhinichthys osculus*), and the arroyo chub (*Gila orcuttii*)." All three occur together only in Big Tujunga Wash above Hansen Dam to about the Big Tujunga Dam upstream (Swift et al., 1993). Rainbow trout, at least partly naturally reproducing, occur here as well but are probably mixed with hatchery stocks. Arroyo chub occur in a few other places such as above Pacoima Reservoir and in the Sepulveda flood control basin. The unarmored threespine stickleback (*Gasterosteus aculeatus williamsoni*), both the migratory and non-parasitic species of lampreys (*Lampetra* spp.), the steelhead trout (*Onchorynchos mykiss*, related to salmon), as well as at least one species of freshwater shrimp have all been gone since the 1930s or '40s (Swift, pers. comm.). Nature as open tomb indeed.

What has come instead? Mutts and goldfish, same as anywhere. The exotics just in Big Tujunga alone include bluegill, green sunfish, threadfin shad, fathead minnow, red shiner, mosquito fish, black bullhead, and, yes, goldfish. In the main river in the Griffith Park area one can find carp, tilapia (*Oreochromis* sp.), and apparently, since the early 1990s, a species of "pleco," referring to the aquarists' shorthand for *Plectostomus*. However, the taxon is actually *Pterygoplichthys* cf. *disjunctivus* according to the authority on these loricariids (suckermouth armored catfishes), a voracious organism endemic to South America and adjacent Central America (*fide* Jonathan Armbruster, Auburn University). They survive the winter by staying in the warm outflows of the Tillman Water Treatment Plant (Swift, pers. comm.). In reservoirs/lakes associated with the lower river it is extremely likely that predictable non-natives such as the redear sunfish, channel catfish, and black crappie occur, and there are a few estuarine invaders like striped mullet, California killifish, topsmelt, staghorn sculpin, and a couple of gobies that could be anticipated in the lowest reaches of the river. "Make it New," the Modernists demanded of all art, but for people in my field, we plead, "Bring back the Originals."

Similarly, although 341 species of birds have been reported historically and collectively from the tributaries and the main course of the Los Angeles River itself (Garrett, 1993), most passerines now are concentrated in patches of successional riparian habitat along the soft-bottomed sections of the river. At one study site near the Glendale Narrows, 116 species have been observed. That tally seems large but isn't—again, with a different choice of management, the river could sponsor a more varied (and more consistently present) avifauna. The occasional sighting of this or that stray migrant does not balance against the loss of an entire community of interlocking species, nor does the establishment of a handful of exotics ("the orange bishops are coming, the orange bishops are coming!") replace the pulsing heart of wild systems.

Backing up now to reiterate a biological truism, in general there is almost always a greater species richness in natural habitats than in disturbed ones. I see this firsthand in my own day-to-day research away from the L.A. River in nearby Orange County. For example, where I teach, roughly 167 species are known from coastal sage scrub habitat on the University of California's Irvine campus, 264 species have been recorded for the adjacent San Joaquin Wetlands, but a meager 40 bird species are commonly found in the eucalyptus and other non-native dominated areas of the campus proper—an 80% decline in 150 years. Our UCI campus mascot is the anteater, which in a way is fitting . . . rats, crows, and ants are about all that are left.

These accounts demonstrate the losses the L.A. River has experienced. Although there is one endangered bird species that still occurs along the River, it does so only in restricted, isolated sites. The Least Bell's Vireo uses the Hansen Dam-Tujunga Wash and Sepulveda Basin Recreation Area, as do several other sensitive species, such as the Yellow-breasted Chat and Blue Grosbeak. The vulnerability of these species was shown recently when a 2007 brush fire burned a great deal of the Hansen Dam habitat.

Yet change is possible. In the words of mad Kit Smart, we should have hope, "for the praise of God can give to a mute fish the notes of a nightingale." Nature may yet sing. The 1993 biota survey reports "a total of 17 species of amphibians and 38 reptiles" from the L.A. River Basin. This includes introduced species such as the common bullfrog, as well as extirpated salamanders and frogs. Yet there is an intact species anthology as close at hand as Big Tijunga

Wash, which means restoration could push species tallies nearly as high as they once were.

Excluding naked bipeds and barking dogs, 38 native mammals were listed in the biota study, plus three non-native species—yes, Virginia, there is a Santa Claus, and he brought us our only marsupial, Opossum, albeit an exotic. Bats and mice and skunks more or less do ok, but the only *Ursos arctos horribilis* still extant waves from the side of the state flag. Want to add your name to the footnotes of science? Motion-sensor cameras could provide a photo essay on bobcats (and homeless people), and in the headwaters, ring-tailed cats awaits study. Lace up your boots and go.

What about plants? Ah, complications there too. The first is a problem of sifting the wheat from the chaff, or more specifically, the natives from the weeds. But what is a weed? As Michael Pollan has summarized in a meditation titled "Weeds Are Us," field guide authors and restoration biologists and Sunday gardeners and Emersonian humanists all differ in their paradigms. One body of thought suggests that a weed is any plant in the wrong place. A narrower, more biological definition is to define a weed as an especially aggressive plant that competes successfully against cultivated plants. Extending that is the notion that weeds are non-native plants displacing native ones, and in so doing, are cheating us of heritage ecosystems.

Let us consider a case in point. In the few areas that were spared hardscaping and still have riparian habitat, the European giant reed (*Arundo donax*) has long been problematic. Basically it looks like a vigorous thicket of bamboo. This pest was not indigenous to the river and so has driven out the "proper" species, and in fact, has been doing so for a long time. According to a state weed study published in the 1930s, "An aged Mexican informed Mr. Lyon that as early as 1820 it was so plentiful along the Los Angeles River that it was gathered for roofing material, for which it was preferred to the tules commonly used for that purpose" (Robbins, Bellyue, and Ball, n.d.). Giant reed flourished along much of the central Santa Ana River, being the dominant vegetation for miles in the Norco and Chino reaches, but has largely been eliminated or reduced during the past decade due to a major eradication program. In many drainages throughout Southern California, homeless people like this hardy plant, since it screens encampments, provides lean-to poles, and cuts a chill winter wind. More dispassionately, thinking about the value to wildlife overall, the usual eco-take is that it is a nuisance plant, sucking up water like crazy and denying the birds their summer holly and seep-willow. In this narrative supposedly few animals even can use arundo, one reason it should be eliminated.

A widdershins view reminds us that "no data" is not "negative data"; according to Jim Greaves, wildlife can and does make use of this cane, at least occasionally, if only we look closely enough. His website documents nesting southwestern willow flycatchers and so on, saying in essence, well, now that giant reed is here, what's so bad about it? I suppose the answer is that having some vegetation, foreign or otherwise, is better than having none at all, but one vision for the L.A. River is a vision of ecological complexity, and that may mean culling some weeds and encouraging others. If so, the cane should go, or some of it anyway. Let future management agencies fight over the exact ratios. It can be a great photo op for some future mayor, down in the river bed with a machete and a *Gran Limpieza* t-shirt, hacking away at the arundo cane, eager to be seen saving the Artemisia and the yellowthroats.

Meanwhile, the rest of the chlorophyll nation carries on, sprouting and budding, blooming and shedding. Considered objectively (and separate from the thick brakes of arundo), the flora of the Los Angeles River is sadly limited, as would be expected in such an artificial, highly disturbed, fragmented site. It may be green and it may be home to sunbursts of goldfinches, but it is not a Noah's Arc of diversity—not yet, anyway. Gary Wallace (in Garrett, 1993) provides an excellent review of historic collections and species summaries for nine areas along the river. As expected, at all of the locations there was a mixture of native and non-native species, as follows: 70% native taxa in Tujunga Wash, 65% natives at Oro Vista, 48% at Newell Street just south of the Fletcher Drive Bridge, and 38% at Willow Creek near Long Beach. Native shrubs occurring at several of these sites included willows, mule fat, cottonwood, ash, and western sycamore. In addition, FoLAR lists include such typical upland species as *Quercus dumosa, Ceanothus cuneatus,* and *Umbellaria california,* enlarging the view to include habitat and species no longer present within the immediate corridor itself, to get us thinking more broadly about the possibilities of restoration plantings to enhance the river's banks and pocket parks.

In the 1993 work, the non-natives include a rogue's gallery of widely spread invasive species, as well as escapees from cultivar settings. Flooding undoubtedly plays a role both in dispersal and scouring of the stands that have become established. In such an unnatural situation it is quite likely that there are many non-native taxa that have colonized since the Natural History Museum's surveys fifteen years ago. That means that just as with bats and other species groups sketched here, much productive and necessary work remains to be done, and therefore this summary might serve better as an invitation than as a definitive position.

Looking Ahead

Anthropocentric uses of the river are many, ranging from bird watching and other recreational appreciation of the surviving riparian fragments, to video games, films, television programs, and music videos that are in some way connected to the river. Particular note should be made of the river's national-caliber gallery of tag art. Once in a great while kayakers are spotted; apparently one trick is to apply for a filming permit, which allows one to trespass throughout Los Angeles under the all-access pass of making moola. (Never enter the river at floodstage, however, or David Quammen will have to write your obituary.) After years of delays, bike and hiking trails now run along some parts of the concrete corridor. Limited equestrian access also exists. If plans move forward, these opportunities are to be expanded, as are parks, and even un-hardscaping and re-establishing riparian vegetation in various sections of the river's course. The heritage of dusty cement will gradually be replaced by ambitious plans to breath life into the phoenix. The evolutionary context cannot be re-created, but there is exciting promise in these highly imaginative, highly necessary restoration plans. Imagination is as important to biology and politics as it is to cinematography and ethnopoetics, and we inhabit a time when we have been granted the chance to apply our full imaginations to this undervalued watercourse. To frame this process, I have been hoarding insights and quotations in my field journal—a collection of found poems and deep ecology wisdom which can serve as epigraphs to action. Any one of these could be outlined in gold and carved over the front doors of City Hall. Taken together, their acts of courage and imagination can sustain and inspire ours.

A Baedeker of Bon Mots

"Inspiration is not garnered from litanies of what is flawed; it resides in humanity's willingness to restore, redress, reform, recover, reimagine, and reconsider. Healing the wounds of the Earth and its people does not require saintliness or a political party. It is not a liberal or a conservative activity. It is a sacred act."

—Paul Hawken, 2007

"A town is saved, not more by the righteous men in it than by the woods and swamps that surround it."

—Henry David Thoreau, 1851

"I agree with Wendell Berry: If we each took care of our home ground (which is an investment in ourselves) the world would be so much better. Why Mars? Know your community, love your community."

—Scott Russell Sanders, 2007

"As a poet I was born in a particular place, a hillside overlooking the Tanana River in central Alaska, where I built a house and lived for the better part of twenty-two years. It was there, in the winter of 1947-1948, that I wrote my first mature poems. Many things went into the making of those poems and the others I've written since: the air of the place, its rocks, soil, and water; snow and ice; human history, birds, animals, and insects. Other things, surely, not directly related to the place: the words of other poets learned once, forgotten, and remembered again. Old stories from childhood, voices out of dreams. Images, a way of seeing learned partly from several years' study as a painter and sculptor. And human relationship, life shared with another person whose existence mingled with my own, so that we saw the world as one person. But it was finally the place itself that provided the means of unifying all of these into a single experience."

—John Haines, 1981

"Nature is not only more complicated than we know, but it is even more complicated than we CAN know."

—Robert Bateman, 1992

"One morning, walking through fresh snow, looking for mountain lion tracks on the north rim of the Grand Canyon, a biologist with years of this behind him said to me suddenly, "It's not in the data." I looked at him. "It's not in the data," he reiterated. With his hands he made a motion to indicate his head, his chest. "It's here. What I know is here." We went on in silence. "But as a field biologist," I said, "you must offer data or ——." "We are not biologists," he answered. "We are historians."

—Barry Lopez, 1983

"Scientific discovery is not a one-way transfer of information from unambiguous nature to minds that are always open. It is a reciprocal interaction between a multifarious and confusing nature and minds sufficiently receptive (as many are not) to extract a weak but sensible pattern from the prevailing noise. There are no signs on the Galápagos that proclaim: EVOLUTION AT WORK. OPEN YOUR EYES AND YE SHALL SEE IT. Evolution is an inescapable inference, not a raw datum. Darwin, young, restless, and searching, was receptive to the signal. Agassiz, committed and defensive, was not. Had he not already announced in the first letter to Pierce that he knew what he must find? I do not think he was free to reach Darwin's conclusions, and the Galápagos Islands, therefore, carried no important message for him. Science is a balanced interaction of mind and nature."

—Stephen Jay Gould, 1985

"And the narrowest hinge in my hand put to scorn all machinery."

—Walt Whitman, 1855

"The environmental crisis is an outward manifestation of a crisis of mind and spirit. There could be no greater misconception of its meaning than to believe it to be concerned only with endangered wildlife, human-made ugliness, and pollution. These are part of it, but more importantly, the crisis is concerned with the kind of creatures we are and what we must become in order to survive."

—Lynton Caldwell, 2003

"One of the penalties of an ecological education is that one lives alone in a world of wounds. Much of the damage inflicted on land is quite invisible to laymen. An ecologist must either harden his shell and make believe that the consequences of science are none of his business, or he must be the doctor who sees the mark of death in a community that believes itself well and does not want to be told otherwise."

—Aldo Leopold, 1953

"If people destroy something replaceable made by mankind, they are called vandals; if they destroy something irreplaceable made by God, they are called Developers."

—Joseph W. Krutch, 1956

"Sustainable development is . . . development that meets the needs of the present without compromising the ability of further generations to meet their own needs."

—World Commission on Environment and Development, 1987

"The success of the scientific method underlines the failure of the political method."

—Bill McKibben, 2003

"Is the base of our history unchanging, like some batholith of sin—are we irretrievable killers?—or can we exist with wolves, this time? I believe we are being given another chance, an opportunity to demonstrate our ability to change. This time, we have a chance to let a swaying balance be struck: not just for wolves, but for humans, too. If I could say any one thing to politicians, and to people with guns and poison (and sheep and cows), it would be this: that to have the balance the majority of people claim to long for, it must be struck by the wolves as much as by the people."

—Rick Bass, 1992

"Under every river is the floor of the world,
and curling downstream a beautiful ribbon
printed with the story
of where water comes from and returns."

—Eloise Klein Healy, 2007

"Travel used to mean exploring a specific location, in a specific season, having the particular experiences in that setting at that moment. But money and technology, it seems, can make geography irrelevant. Wealthy people in developed nations have become so accustomed to having whatever they want whenever they want it—watermelon in winter, Italian food in Japan—that place and time are becoming vague concepts for a lot of vacationers. . . . It's July on the Arabian Peninsula . . . but Ski Dubai has five downhill runs, a snow cave, two après-ski cafés. They'll even rent you an overcoat. Just don't examine the illusion too closely, or you'll see that the starry sky overhead is a painted ceiling with electric lights. We want adventures without surprises, gratification without delay. And for a price, we [think we] can have it all."

—Reiner Ridelder, 2007

"Magic, then, in its perhaps most primordial sense, is the experience of existing in a world made up of multiple intelligences, the intuition that every form one perceives—from the swallow swooping overhead to the fly on a blade of grass, and indeed the blade of grass itself—is an experiencing form, an entity with its own predilections and sensations, albeit sensations that are very different from our own."

—David Abram, 1996

"[Being read to at age eight] I found *Sand County Almanac* boring. Only a grownup writing for grownups would describe wild geese and say nothing about wanting to fly away with them. Nature was magic, real magic, and good books were magic too. My brothers and sisters must have felt the same as I did, because the next evening my mother switched to *Alice in Wonderland*."

—George Gessert, 2007

"All which isn't singing is mere talking."

—e.e. cummings, 1932

Where We Are Now (Is Not Where We Will Be)

Like a self-consuming cancer we have the ability to swallow ourselves—no need to seek lost feelings by swallowing it in San Juan; we have done it to the Los Angeles River without outside help. Though more Steinbeck than Stegner, a kind of geography of hope still lives at least in the headwaters of the Los Angeles River, and those mountains are not at an angle of repose. Through stint and with broken flow, the Los Angeles River slips from its modern past toward a different created state of augmentation. Obviously it can never be returned to any true form of pre-disturbance state; nonetheless, its harmed soul can be remediated in many ways, and manufactured into a far greater ecological resource than it is today. Silt fills dams to their brims in time, while water eats away at foundation joints. Changes come, whether we want them to or not. (To our east, its impoundments silting up even faster than predicted, the Grand Canyon casts a slow smile at the dams to come down.) Just as a deliberately scuttled aircraft carrier can sustain the preliminary workings of a coral reef, or just as mines and mine tailings can be induced to sustain ecology, so can a concrete gash in the landscape. Kerouac has said that "nothing is muddy that runs in time and to the laws of time." The Friends of the Los Angeles River ask us to imagine "a healthy Los Angeles River . . . a greenway of parks from the mountains to the sea . . . a river of students learning science and history in the field . . . people making a difference in their neighborhoods . . . a river with a voice . . . and a swimable, fishable, boatable Los Angeles River." May the gods bless Lewis MacAdams and all other visionary warriors.

FoLAR's long-term goals include "eliminating pollution and restoring the river's natural habitat; applying modern flood-protection technologies that are aligned with a healthy ecosystem; encouraging appropriate uses of reclaimed water for irrigation and recharge of the aquifers."

The Los Angeles River Revitalization Master Plan, unveiled February 2, 2007, proposes the first cohesive vision for the kinds of goals forwarded by FoLAR. The revitalization plan proposes 239 projects—primarily parks—along 32 miles of the river from Canoga Park to Los Angeles at an estimated price of $2 billion, to be implemented within the next 25 to 50 years. According to the *Los Angeles Times* (Feb. 2), ". . . the plan is significant not for its specifics but for its sweep and boldness in proposing to turn the industrial strength storm drain running from the San Fernando Valley to the sea into 'one of the city's most treasured landmarks.'" Though most of the new amenities are small pocket parks, two parks near Chinatown and Canoga Park are quite large and will incorporate residential and office villages, replacing the existing factories and warehouses. The river would be widened in places to continue its flood control mission, while allowing the return of riparian habitat.

The City of Los Angeles, the U.S. Army Corps of Engineers, and their associated consultants created the plan, not yet funded. River restoration in cities and urban settings has come of age, and there are many biocentric as well as anthropocentric rationales for the revitalization plan.

Please see Table 4.

Table 4. Five "areas of opportunity" for enriching new habitat for human users and wildlife. An identified challenge is coping with the railroad tracks that run along the river—by working around, over, or under them. (Excerpted and adapted from the *Los Angeles Times*, February 2, 2007. Original source Los Angeles River Revitalization Master Plan.)

Key Provisions of the L. A. River Revitalization Master Plan
• **Governance**: The plan calls for three new agencies to guide river restoration. One would be a joint powers authority of city and county officials to oversee construction, while the other two would be nonprofits that focus on managing the land and fundraising. • **Water Quality**: Several solutions are posed to help clean polluted water that spills into the river from storm drains. Most proposals would rely on filtering the water through new tributary and main course vegetation before it reaches the river. • **Location**: Many projects are targeted for one of five areas determined last year: the river's headwaters in Canoga Park; the confluence of the river and the Verdugo Wash near Griffith Park; the new Taylor Yard State Park next to Cypress Park; Chinatown; and the river between the Santa Ana and Santa Monica freeways.
The Los Angeles River's Five "Areas of Opportunity":
• **Canoga Park**: The plan envisions several blocks of parks and new housing immediately east of the confluence of Calabasas and Bell Creeks, where the Los Angeles River begins. • **River Glen (at Griffith Park)**: A park, with wetlands, would be constructed under the Ventura Freeway where a newly-landscaped Verdugo Wash spills into the Los Angeles River. • **Taylor Yard**: The plan envisions widening the river and creating wetlands and wildlife habitat. • **Chinatown-Cornfield area**: A new park would be linked to the river with green space and a second channel through the park. • **Downtown industrial area**: The stretch between the Santa Ana and Santa Monica freeways would be heavily landscaped with native riparian vegetation.

Small initial projects include constructing signature pedestrian bridges and the completion of a bike path from Chinatown to Griffith Park along the river's edge. Bringing people closer to the river is a large theme in the new plan. The plan calls for widening and deepening the river corridor, thus improving riparian conditions while still allowing the flood control capacity to function. At many sites concrete is proposed to be removed and the channel will be expanded and riparian habitat will be allowed to develop. This is not dehumanized or without political reality; the plan projects 6,200 new residential units near Canoga Park and 4,665 residences adjacent Chinatown. By carefully implementing the plan over a long period of time through private and public funding, the approach is one that is being followed in river restoration not only at many sites in North America, but also in Australia and other countries. It *can* work; it must be allowed to work.

As Australian restorationist Sam Day stated, "For us to succeed in either restoration ecology or the practice of ecological restoration we need politicians, management agencies, and research institutions to think in the long term." The Los Angeles River has that kind of support now, and the "one piece at a time" approach, like Johnny Cash's Cadillac, will yield a cumulative and synergistic product over time. We have cause for hope.

Table 5. An anthology of values associated with wetlands, including wild and restored settings. (Adapted from Nash, 1978)

- **Normal ecological processes**—"Wild places take on importance as models of ecological balance and land health. They constitute a criterion against which to measure the impact of civilization."
- **Crucible of the American Character**—"America's natural resources have helped shape the American character. The recognition that space—emptiness, solitude, wilderness, and vast unmodified distances—is the distinguishing element in the American experience is widely shared. The environment of origin is clearly important in defining and sustaining national character . . . 'something will have gone out of us as a people if we ever let the remaining wilderness be destroyed . . . if we drive the few remaining members of the wild species into zoos or to extinction' (Wallace Stegner, 1960)."
- **Creativity**—There is a connection between natural states or undisturbed situations (wildness) and creativity.
- **Historical Document**—The landscape or natural resource is a historical document that "... can reveal, more dramatically than conventional records, how people felt."
- **Danger and Challenge**—"In wild places humans learn to live with danger again."
- **Freedom, Individual Dignity, and Human Diversity**—Nash calls wildness and the idea of wilderness part of the geography of hope. "The role of wildness in advancing social and intellectual diversity is just becoming apparent. We understand the incompatibility of wildness with totalitarian systems where everything is controlled and there is no place to hide."
- **Religion**—"For example, Colin Fletcher says that in wilderness 'you regain a sense of harmony with everything you move through . . . you are part of the great web of life...you know the wholeness of the universe . . . the great unity.' John Muir had the same reaction; for him a wilderness trip was an act of worship."
- **Mental Health**—"Wilderness activities put humans back in touch with their biological roots and provide a chance for self-sufficiency that civilization has destroyed." It satisfies the need to "get away from it all."
- **Education for Environmental Responsibility**—"Values, attitudes and priorities are at the core of the environmental crisis ... Wilderness can also teach that community is a concept that does not end with man or what he controls."
- **Because It Is There**—"The wild world is good for itself, good, that is, just because it exists."

In many ways, attempts to deconstruct the L.A. River's role as civilization's sacrificial lamb is an act that reflects deep ecology—the philosophical grounding that considers the intrinsic value of the L.A. River in and unto itself. Rocks, landscapes, and ecosystems have often been accorded rights, and in a subtle way, we are remembering the intrinsic right of the L.A. River to exist—and at the same time, feeling better about our re-play of history, with a corrected ending. The immediate beneficiaries of an ecologically-upgraded L.A. River are wildlife, but human beneficiaries are in the line already. In a sense we are remembering our own personal, cultural, and evolutionary contexts—and want to re-populate the grave. Urban restorations are valuable on many levels—initially for the wildlife that will inhabit them but ultimately for humans as well. The natural arteries to the sea still reach it through the cracks of modernity, and there are plans in place to widen the course here, remove the heavy concrete jacket there, and upgrade the habitats (riparian and otherwise) that struggle at its edge. We now know and have the ability—and will—to reawaken many echoes and re-discover a shadow of the floodplain dance this river once executed.

By doing these stair step, progressive small projects, there will be a cumulative lifting of the ecological condition of the river, and the species richness from birds to vascular plants will rebound, just as it is along the Owens River, to our north. And so will a new appreciation of the river as an integrated anthropocentric/biocentric experience for humans. Restoration can be a resurrection of what has been viewed as a closed case. John McPhee gave us a magnificent telling of the ultimate folly of our attempting to control the sheddings of the San Gabriel Range in those steep and rising mountains. The floodplain confluences of the Los Angeles and San Gabriel Rivers are harnessed in stopgap debris traps from headwaters to floodplain, but the promise of pardon in many areas of the floodplain allows hope and shows commitment to the restoration of what can be retrieved.

As Wallace Stegner put it so nicely when discussing Wendell Berry in *A Sense of Place*,

> If you don't know where you are you don't know who you are. He is not talking about the kind of location that can be determined by looking at a map or a street sign. He is talking about the kind of knowing that involves the senses, the memory, the history of a family or a tribe. He is talking about the knowledge of place that comes from working in it in all weathers, making a living from it, suffering from its catastrophes, loving its mornings or evenings or hot noons, valuing it for the profound investment of labor and feeling that you, your parents and grandparents, your all-but-unknown ancestors have put into it. He is talking about the knowing that poets specialize in.
>
> It is only a step from his pronouncement to another: that no place is a place until it has had a poet. And that is about what Yeats was saying only a moment ago. No place, not even a wild place, is a place until it has had that human attention that at its highest reach we call poetry. What Frost did for New Hampshire and Vermont, what Faulkner did for Mississippi, and Steinbeck for the Salinas Valley, Wendell Berry is doing for his family corner of Kentucky, and hundreds of other place-loving people, gifted or not, are doing for places they were born in, or reared in, or have adopted and made their own.

As this present text so delightfully demonstrates, Bruce Bartrug and Charles Hood are doing this for the Los Angeles River. Other artists parallel them. In recent fine art photography we can think about the excellent river and cityscape work being done by Michael Light and David Maisel, John Humble and Anthony Hernandez, Douglas Hill and Mark Lamonica. There are the river gate sculptures of Brett Goldstone and panorama murals of tagging which combine stylized Mayan flourishes with the vivid colors of the Apocalypse. While perhaps in the past art has been too slow to find the river, what is obvious is that the renaissance is in full chorus now.

Jenny Price (2007) summarizes it best. "L.A.'s errant treatment of a major natural feature has profoundly exacerbated nearly all of L.A.'s notorious troubles—environmental chaos, social inequities, community fragmentation, water shortages, water imperialism, and erasure of civic memory. The good news, on the other hand, is that by using and managing . . . nature more sustainably and fairly, we can make the city a healthier, more equitable, and all-around lovelier place to live in. First, though, you have to see the nature in the place. You have to find it." Angelenos have found nature peeking out from beneath a concrete skirt and they want to see more. They want to see it dance, sing, and howl at a grizzly California moon. Let us join them.

References and Literature Cited

Bowler, PA. 1988. "Thoughts about Subtle Impact Potentials of Headwater Sited Small Hydroelectric Developments on River Processes." pp 13–18 in Bradley, E. (ed.). *Proceedings of the State of the Sierra Symposium*, 1985–86. Pacific Publications Co., San Francisco, California.

Brownlie, W.R. and B.D. Taylor. 1981. *Sediment Management for Southern California Mountains, Coastal Plains, and Shoreline.* Calif. Inst. Technol. EQL Rep. 17-C. 314 pp.

California Coastal Conservancy. *Wetland Profile: Los Angeles River.* http//www.scc.ca.gov.

Cameron, R. 1980. *Above Los Angeles*. Fifth Printing. Cameron and Company, San Francisco, California.

Carle, D. 2000. *Water and the California Dream: Choices for the New Millennium*. Sierra Club Books, San Francisco, California.

Cummins, K.E., C.E. Cushing and G.W. Minshall. 1995. "Introduction: An Overview of Stream Ecosystems." Pp. 1–8. In*:* Cushing, C.E. , K.W. Cummins, and G.W. Minshall. *Ecosystems of the World 22: River and Stream Ecosystems*. Elsevier, Amsterdam, The Netherlands.

Davis, M. 1998. *Ecology of Fear: Los Angeles and the Imagination of Disaster.* Vintage Books (Random House), New York, New York.

Deverell, W. (ed). 2005. *Land of Sunshine: An Environmental History of Metropolitan Los Angeles*. University of Pittsburgh Press, Pittsburgh, Pennsylvania.

Faber, P.M., E. Keller, A. Sands, and B.M. Massey. 1989. *The Ecology of Riparian Habitats of the Southern California Coastal Region: a Community Profile*. Biological Report 85(7.27). U.S. Department of the Interior, Fish and Wildlife Service,

Research and Development, National Wetlands Research Center, Washington, D.C. 20240.

Fox, W. 2007. *Making Time: Essays on the Nature of Los Angeles*. Shoemaker Hoard, Emeryville, California.

Garrett, K.L. (ed.). 1993. *The Biota of the Los Angeles River*. Natural History Museum of Los Angeles County Foundation, for the California Department of Fish and Game.

Gumprecht, B. 2001. *The Los Angeles River: Its Life, Death, and Possible Rebirth*. Johns Hopkins University Press, Baltimore, Maryland.

Linton, J. 2005. *Down by the Los Angeles River*. Wilderness Press, Berkeley, California.

MacAdams, L. 2005. *The River: Books One, Two, & Three*. Blue Press, Santa Cruz, California.

McDonald, T. 2007. "Visions of stream restoration; the need for long-term, big-picture projects: Interview with Sam Lake." *Ecological Management and Restoration* 8(1): 5–10.

McPhee, J. 1989. *The Control of Nature*. Farrar Strauss Giroux, New York, New York.

Morrison, P., and M. Lamonica. 2001. *Río L.A.: Tales from the Los Angeles River*. Angel City Press, Santa Monica, California.

Nash, R. 1982. *Wilderness and the American Mind*. Yale University Press, New Haven, Connecticut.

———. 1978. "Who Loves a Swamp?" National Symposium on Strategies for Protection and Management of Floodplain Wetlands and Other Riparian Ecosystems.

Petts, G. and P. Calow (eds.). 1996. "River Restoration." Selected extracts from *The Rivers Handbook*, Blackwell Science, Boston, Massachusetts.

Price, J. 2007. "Writer's Block." *Conservation Magazine* 8(2): 28–34. (April–June 2007 issue).

Quammen, D. 1998. *Wild Thoughts from Wild Places*. Scribner, New York, New York.

Quinn, R. and S. Keeley. 2006. *Introduction to California Chaparral*. University of California Press, Berkeley, California.

Robbins, W.W., M.K. Bellue, and W.S. Ball. n.d. *Weeds of California*. California State Department of Agriculture, Sacramento, California.

Starr, K. 2005. *California: A History*. The Modern Library, New York, New York.

Swift, C. C., T. R. Haglund, M. Ruiz, and R. N. Fisher. 1993. "The Status and Distribution of Freshwater Fishes of Southern California." *Bull. Southern California Acad. of Sci.* 92(3): 101–167.

Vannote, R.L., G.W. Minshall, K.W. Cummins, J.R. Sedell, and C.E. Cushing. 1980. "The River Continuum Concept." *Can. J. Fish. Aquat. Sci.* 37: 130–137.

Water from Stone

by Bruce Bartrug

I have worn parrot plumes
musk cat skins
I have exhausted the missionaries' patience.

—Aimé Césaire

Los Angeles River
TOW-AWAY
NO STOPPING
ANY TIME
BAB07

BAB07

BAB07

BAB07

BAB07

Harder Than Light

by Charles Hood

Understanding consists in the reduction of one type of reality to another, and that the true reality is never the most obvious.

—Claude Lévi-Strauss, *Tristes tropiques*

Mal Sueño

"Landscape only *seems* innocuous."
—Mark Klett at the Getty, 2006

In the eager rain of an El Niño dawn
a thousand waterfalls wait to pour red mud
into the open mouths of bedroom and slab,
pool deck and spa tub, mud that will thread
oak trees through Cadillacs, wiping toyon clean
with the hem of a prom dress and the bent rod
from front room drapes and a dozen newly
peeled slabs of Irish-green, laid-by-amigos
sod. That will be the first step. Second,
after the fires and earthquakes, will be to
pick up the river and give it a slap like a
rope trick, a wrist-flipped ripple to lift
and shift and snap the bed out to full length,
letting it be a river and not flood control's
stone barn. Alders will bud as black rails call;

new condors will hunch like winos in the rain.
When the levees fail and Lakewood looks like
the Lower Ninth Ward, nobody will say, as most
do now, *what, Los Angeles has a river?* Name it
ecology's last dibs when even Bill Mulholland
will have to ride sidesaddle over the passes
and into the valley of the shadow of the death
of nitgrass and broomrape, pickleweed and galled
oak limb. The cowled gull wheels; surging water
low-bids cement even in summer; retaining walls
can't hold back the pressing fingertips of history.
Tag while you can, happy vatos. Sniff glue,
watch those poorer than you do laundry in the
shiny runoff from the Lockheed parking lot.
We will all be gabachos in Heaven. And when
a hundred-year rain storm brings Los Angeles
a thousand-year flood, look up at the mountains
and curse the men who told us to live on the sodden
plains of Eden, and not, instead, amid the granite
and agave and lightning spikes of the tallest, safest,

hardest places. In 1700 the Chumash mended nets,
rode out the hard rains, moved like the antelope
from ciénega to ciénega, from salmon to cielo.
By 1800 smallpox had come and gone, meaning
there were too many horses, not enough cattle,
so the extra horses were rounded up and driven
off the seacliffs to die smashed on low tide rocks.
It was a hard thing to be Spanish, and by 1900
reduced to begging work and living in Niggertown,
harder still. Paving the channel saved the mortgages
of the brown people owned by red brick banks
and if the steelhead stopped running, so what,
go to Seattle and get more, and bring back some
2 x 4s while you're at it. Adobe is an archaeology
of transubstantiation: just mud and straw, but the
clay came from the body of Christ of the Past Floods
and coring the binder reveals the pollen of the grasses
that kept coming back after the first grasses couldn't
come back anymore: cheatgrass and Russian thistle
instead of the bunched rice grasses that could feed a city

of deer, an empire of ants, a river of red-winged blackbirds.
Now it just gets stuck in the socks of the kids cutting
across the vacant lot on their way to ESL lessons
or to take abuelita to Our Lady of the Angels
for Sunday mass; the grass spikes are from Europe
and the socks are from Wal-Mart, and in Frogtown,
1968, when the cholos said *Hey Paddy, gimme your*
watch or I will break your arm, I wanted to say back,
no, not 'Paddy,' since Irish is the one indentured heritage
I am not, or maybe, *what, you can tell time now?*
But I didn't, I just gave them my watch and went
to sulk down by cat-faced storm drains grinning
from slab sides of a river that is in the background
of the chase scenes in *Laurel and Hardy*, *Keystone Cops*,
Grease. *Around the World in 80 Days* was backlotted
by Stage 27, look for the river as the balloon rises.
Some days even movies cannot save us my mother said,
sending me to Saul's market for a fist of ground-round
in white paper. Kids never know what the hell grownups
are talking about, and thank god for small favors. Now

the river has bird guides, hiking books, but you can still
score blow or find a dumb white kid to rob, or shoot up
two rolls of Nikon trying to get the heron backlit just so.
Sycamores push against chainlink as green glass glints
under the feet of the mayor's urban renewal task force.
Clipboards nod as hardhats talk. A pale red-tail hovers,
hoping to nail a gimp rat by the underpass. I-5 hums.
After the next flood the walls will be higher, towers
will be built with sirens and webcams for high water,
ducks will nest on roofs for a season or two while FEMA
fucks around, trying to decide what to do. Ten years ago
when a man was going to commit suicide, his '72 Impala
was stolen while he stood by the river, and he was so mad
he couldn't do it. He did though shoot a carjacker later
and now he is in Twin Towers, vexed to suicide's edge
once more. Metrolink's white cars parallel the Narrows
and if you have sex on the train the fine is $1000. People
still raise chickens, stir cinnamon molé, take swings
at each other on Sunday. What the river is now waits
for what it will be soon enough, ready and angry

and a kind of wet fist in the mouth of inevitability.
Look—somebody is taking a photograph of a single
red shoe, as sad as offramp veterans or a wedding dress
on eBay. The poet walks, writing, thinking about
how you can name the rocks after the saints and
yet still spend half an inheritance on riprap
and debris basins. Blame it on the blue herons'
rickrack nest mounds. Blame the eco-nuts. Time now
to round up the Japanese and put them in camps
again, or is it the towelheads we are after this time,
anything to keep the lamps lit and streets safe.
Raccoons eat catfood in the dark; a shirtless man
hand-lines carp. He will die when it rains but for now
his scrap twig fire smells like Yosemite and soy sauce,
not so different from the Gabrielino village this river
washed the feet of three hundred years ago. *Acorns
look like a woman's nipples*, he thinks, cooking another fish.
The moon in the water is just trying to look under her skirt.
In Los Angeles the bridges have better architecture
than the churches. When the rivers are all gone,

where will the clouds go to hold hands? *Agua bendita,*
río de reinas y ruidosos, río flaco seco. River of holy water,
river of queens and kickboxers, skinny dried-up river.
Rivers should not be square. Imagine instead terraced houses,
smell the melon slices cooling on ceramic plates, hear cold water
sliding over weir and sluicegate. No, look—the pepper tree rusts
in a sunset as red as the shimmer of oil leaking out of an overturned
Peterbilt. It didn't have to be this way. "No Dumping: This Drain
Drains Into the Ocean." Save the fish. Save the fish taco vendor
going home to a nine hundred square foot house painted lime green
behind the black iron bars of fear's guitar. At Allesandro Street
a car has endo'd over the bank, gone into the river; its taillights
glow like two retro-rockets aimed for the center of the earth.
Power lines sway in hot air. Willows and pampas grass burn
with incandescent fungus. Yellow strings of parasitic weeds
drape the shopping cart like tired moss. Mallards wage war
on grass. Your friend says, "looks like somebody built it here,
just decided to install a river." Feral parrots burst past overhead,
late for evening roosts. Homeless people have one kind of uniform,
the horse people, another. Joggers slug electrolytes from neon bottles.

Chopper Air Ten-Seventy swings low, ready to transmogrify the dead
semi into the stations of the SigAlert. *There should be a kind of polo
they play using helicopters*, the writer thinks, then adds that
too, sketching a flock of Blackhawks circling palm trees
in the sinking light, waiting for the next burst of words
to jitter out of his mouth like bats, singing a sad song
from *Love Song for Bobbie Long* about Washboard Lisas,
singing as he imagines meanly the flood to come,
singing for the night herons and harvest mice,
singing a nonsense river song,
singing while he waits.

Where to Put Things

Things to put on the banks of the L.A. River, 1769-1969: The orphanage, the dog pound, the stock yards, the slaughterhouse, the city dump, the city jail, the county jail, the INS jail, the sewage works, the meat packing plant, the pulp paper mill, the target range, Chinatown, Koreatown, Niggertown, the morgue, gasoline storage tanks, and the pauper's cemetery. *Things not to put on the banks of the L.A. River* (ask Mr. Baldwin, whose scallop-shingled mansion washed away in the floods of 1885): the houses of the rich people.

Notes for a Haiku Cycle about the City on Fire:

something here about the inevitable fires of late summer
when the Santa Ana winds incinerate hope and moderation
then we need a political reference to Chavez Ravine,
evictions, poor people, chaparral ready to burn—

then end with the way the brush fire's flames look,
upside-down,

reflected in water.

THE HISTORY OF L.A. AS TOLD THROUGH A TIME-LAPSE PHOTOGRAPH in reverse order describing what happens when Beck flushes his toilet in Silverlake:

unjiggle the handle, ballcock and float rise to full, the water flowing backwards through the house walls, left turn then right turn and out to the main, a hidden river of water certified clear and pure rushing backwards to the DWP treatment plant the EPA testing shuttlecock valve the coiled hoses the OSHA approved stainless steal aeration chamber bending up and through standpipe past bolted flange shunt valve through deep tanks underground then more black pipes then the calm green eye of the final reservoir open to the sky under moonlight and the moon is its perfect reverse pupil tonight but the water again is rushing now back up the far end of the Valley into the aqueduct and tunnels backwards through San Fernando Agua Dulce Palmdale Mojave going back up the creosote sides of the Southern Sierra Nevada past the turnoff to Cal City, Jawbone Canyon, the Honda test track, first sagebrush then the cinder cones and clean black basalt cliffs of Little Lake, past petroglyphs and campsites at Fossil Falls, the Cartago spill gate running slow at 134 cubic feet per second then up and passing Big Pine and Caltech's calm rational all-white radio telescopes searching the sky above the horizon line of the White Mountains' bristlecones, water remembering the stones of Manzanar, by-passing Bishop, chilled water mingling with the warmer layers of the intermediate storage reservoirs as a Swainson's hawk glides past on a storm front smelling richly of new-mown alfalfa, up past Owens Gorge and Crowley Lake until it branches off over a final small dam below Lee Vining and rises steadily up willow alder aspen cottonwood side canyon streambed and the trout are dark-eyed blurs as it races past them and up higher higher to the smallest crease in the drainage line at the highest cirque in the springmelt Sierra, high high up, so high and steep and the water now is coalescing into slush, thawing, refreezing, climbing out of the couloirs onto flanking snowpack, ice crystals locking and unlocking like the fingers of the child's hands, here is the church, here is the steeple, open the doors and see all the people, only each of the little faces in the church is white and frost-edged, snow mouths and snow noses in dancing circles on small and perfect snow faces, all of them staring upwards in praise, staring upwards and standing up now, standing up and singing and stretching their robed arms and rising in ascending swirls, rising, rising, the beads of water small as the microscopic pointed tips of feathers, rising upwards into a gun metal light, little white hummingbirds of water rising up out of sight into the clench and release of a dark winter sky.

Joy Ride (1)

"Even when an angel makes you fly, you are the wings."
—Lyn Hejinian

Cars don't need us
but do like to watch us, the dead, wave like flags,
can't wait to hear what our colors will be this year,
what sex will be done where. *Backdoor.* I grew
hard of hearing at the drag races, admired Rat Fink,
liked to misconstrue *flew the coupe* and *double headers.*
To remember growing up is to remember old cars:
yellow on black number plates, space-wand curb feelers,
paired lunchbox speakers at the drive-in—see how the sky
in the movies rests so lightly on the steering wheel,
quiet rectangles of static light. Do you make good
three point turns? Driver's license as birth certificate—
as Wanda Coleman says, to drive is to live. The last
hitchhiker I picked up, twenty years ago this spring,
I stopped for just before the 4th Street Bridge. Thin,

head a little too big like a character in Thunderbirds,
dirty hair, a model's lips. Just waking up each day
is a blind date with hope. I was going to work,
had in my new earring, while he had busy eyes,
a transistor radio, a bent stiletto, and a grudge
against traffic. He was entirely on the side
of the cars, he explained, because traffic made
them want to stab something. Chernobyl
was two days away. He rubbed the knife
on the seat, blade flat. The car turned to glass,
the road as well, both of us going 35 transparent
miles per hour, me miming a casual U-turn, him
rubbing a knife in circles on invisible fabric.
We could look down, see the river far below,
look ma, I have wings. If you could have just
one super power, would you rather be invisible
or would you rather fly, would you rather
love that which will never be able to love
back, or would you want to see the future,
stop the reactor from melting down, the

baby from unlatching the pool gate, the
knife from prying open the head's bones
like the lid of a wet, stuck jar? They say it
just looked like regular smoke, Chernobyl,
even as birds dropped from the sky, a day
like any other. My hitchhiker turns to stare,
complains he can hear the other cars talking
about us, and they do not like my driving.
Thank you, Jesus, but this one you can love
for me. I pull over in a red zone, turn off
the key, take it out, put it in my shirt pocket,
lift up my door lock, flip on the hazards,
and walk away, just leaving him sitting in
an invisible car miles above a shoelace river.
Maybe the angels can use his hair for nests;
maybe he has not one but three or four powers;
maybe he can jump down and fly through the
floor of the bridge. Later I drove home the slow
way, taking hours, my hand tracing where
the knife had been, massaging the seat,

leaving the radio on even during commercials,
making each turn with exaggerated care,
thinking about the abyss that is each person
and what winds blow up out of them,
the rare times when we step up to the edge
and lean over
                                        and look all the way down.

Joy Ride (2)

Both doors off, rotors warming up, cameras set. Mickey Mouse headphones pinch ears. Then no soundtrack, no bon voyage from the crowd, just some acronyms with the tower and then we do not start flying it is just that the ground falls away, body as halo, glass bubble rising through ceilings of light. Hover in place while pilot remembers to put on his seatbelt, chastised by the tower because they could see it dangling free out the open side as we held steady, fifty feet up. Higher and north now as horizon swings like a compass bubble, banking past the Queen Mary to pull straight up the main channel, upstream from tide and harbor as the river bottom thins out into broad green algae patterns, a Versailles of moss, against which little exploding flocks of birds catch the light, drop into shadow, reignite five feet higher. Reference points dissolve trying to tell the gulls from the trash, is that somebody's sleeping head or is it a pirate's spilled spray of pearls. Eyes burn; moss is gorgeous plush. Cross wires dance in Santa Anas and slanted light. A trailer park is laid out in a concentric circle, Stonehenge doublewides, all worshipping Rec Hall center point. Open cockpit: don't drop anything. We pivot in place as I change film and try to find the trick to stay lucid, sober, to be science, to be that which observes, memorizes, writes, names, counts.

Counting ibis in a patterned flock, counting the number of red cars crossing a bridge like jaunty bugs, counting the different layers of river water, deeper medial channel scored straight down the centerline, dissection point to divide the quadrants of the torso. Air is layers of hot, cold, hot, and the wind keeps catching in my mouthpiece, burns the intercom with afterburner static until the pilot turns me off. Leaning out to shoot, slipstream velocity pushes back my face into cartoon grimace. Wind lifts my camera straps off my head, tangles them in the headphone wires, so I wrap them around my fists like boxing tape. Traffic and trains right angle across the anonymous river, the only space with no billboards. Clear view of hulky, corrugated mountains, clusters of downtown high-rises scuffling around like kids nervous in a new school, afraid to look in the eyes of the barrios hemmed up on all sides. Lozenges of swimming pools start appearing near Glendale, run all the way to Chatsworth, lagoon blue and blister perfect. A magnolia tree blossoms in points of white fire. Palm trees burn from below as the first sodium vapor lamps switch on. False-fronted house roofs: red tile up to the streetside peak then flat grey tarpaper. Blinking headlights of LAPD response car, radio traffic on the headset, our helicopter handed off from control to control, freeways open in one direction, slow in another. Crossing Griffith Park to detour to the Hollywood Sign and back, flushing two brush-brown mule deer. Paths and trails through the chaparral rush into view, drop away, too slow to keep up. Shutters in synch at a thousandth of a second, shoot the sign then turn around back to the grid lines of the river, back to Spearmint Rhino billboards, container trucks parking, railroad tracks laid out like wiring blueprints, small strands uniting into thicker bundles. Changing film again, pilot trying to hold my side steady downwind, like a bigger horse trying to protect a smaller one in a snowy wind. The river is less lush from the air, more constrained, its willows and feeder storm drains looking trivial, almost frivolous among T-square commerce. In Atwater I think I can see a house I used to live in, a bar, then a market, then can see roller-bladers, can see tarp villages sprawling inside a palisade of arundo cane. Golden light of the hills, not from the west but lit from within, rows of newly framed houses, more swimming pools backed right up to the edge of the river. If we had planned it differently the river here could have been Malibu, riverfront property looking out over green water and punt docks, Meg Ryan seen walking a Pomeranian past that new place that is so popular for brunch. Maybe we would rather have the homeless. Now it is furniture factories and parking for the Metro line. Houses, streets, schools—are people so bad? How can a city be more than one block after the other? Grids crossing grids: transmission lines have right of way, diagonal paths keeping olive drab strips of dirt open for community gardens and potted eucalyptus rows and then other parts bare, locked, off limits. We swing past the west edge of Chatsworth Reservoir: end of the line: upstream is just cirrus and sky and Lexus brakelights winding through the passes. Water from stone. The river has headwaters in Rocketdyne, Stony Point, Calabasas. There were Nike missile bunkers here in the 1950s, probably still are. Scabs of dry hills too tough to admit that they miss the springs that made the streams that made the rivers. They know they do not have to wait long and the water will be back. This earthquake or the next, one mayor or another. Fires will clear the houses, the brush will burn, regrow, burn, grow again. The water will be back. Afternoon grows late and we have overstayed fuel's welcome. Throttle open we cross the Valley, quick detour to shoot the Getty, UCLA, the Playboy Mansion. The 10 looks bad tonight. Quiet by Signal Hill: no gas flares over the refineries in Wilmington. The sea is dark. We can see the airfield, tower clearing us to land. The first evening fog is forming as we cross PCH just above a park, no it is a cemetery, the helicopter pushing a lane through the cooling air as I rewind the film and nod at the pilot and a blanket of thin mist pulls itself up the chins of the speeding graves and falls away behind.

Bestiary

Algae looks like a big green mess even to the museum botanists
which is why they stir an eddy full of goober weed
and lift it up on a stick like overcooked snot pasta
and say *Hocus pocus deleriums* and *Aphasia borealis*
of the substrata Rumpwhistle, and then run off
laughing like Long Dong when he is drunk
at the end of *Sixteen Candles*. Not that they
do, really, at least not in the algae chapter
of *Biota of the Los Angeles River*, but o
how we want them to, damn how
we need them to.

B is for boys and boys do nasty things. What if we made a river
and left all of the boys
out of it?

Choral swirls of *a cappella* color limn the migration
of the butterflies, see them see them now

lie on your back and focus binoculars
as if looking past the sky to a new sky
one layer back, lie on the bank flat out
and rack the focus near-to-far and farther,
it goes all the way up, they are butterflies
no they are colors migrating from tree to tree
no they are the torn pages
                    of very small books.

Write, *desire.* Write, *he desired her.* He desired her
    sister more than her but her water broke
    his eyes, the water of her hair reaching
    the smooth stones of her shoulders
    poured into him, filled him pure
    so with desire that he could not
    love her, it was too much, she
    was too much, he desired her
    sister in exchange, the way
    that the jaguar, on display,
    walks every day, devouring
    the shadows of the bars

with each obsessive
and insatiable
step.

Even the endemic ants, the termites. Even the ship-borer worms.
Even them.

If flowers have a language—pink carnation, *I'll never forget you,*
purple hyacinth, *the slow acid wash of lingering sorrow*—
what can be done here, land of pampas grass (*your hair*
is very bushy today) or burr-sage or the water pepper and
Bermuda grass—*my love for you sends runners, can even*
crack the driveway. The willow dock greets each sunrise
shuttered by blueweed and cocklebur. Weeping lovegrass
thrives. Sedge blooms under mule fat. Be like the fennel,
only useful when crushed. Jimsonweed datura says that
your body is just a smock to wear while painting the rooms
of your life; when you finish, turn off the music, step back,
say, well now,
that doesn't look so bad.

Grasshoppers are (or, mostly, were) the bison of California floodplain.
Because the kingbirds couldn't keep up and because insects are female
Figueroa and Fourth was called *Calle de las Chapules*, grasshopper street.
Better to live there than the part of Boyle Heights known as *Las Pulgas*,
the fleas, o mama, the fleas.

Homo sapiens: humans, people. Distinguished from the Pongidae (gorillas)
primarily by an angel-wing pelvis and the elongated femurs
required by bipedalism. From *Pan troglodytes*, chimpanzee,
by the fact that we do not eat termites from a stick
though once in the Amazon I ate *hormigas de límon*,
lemon ants, live from a vine. They were sugar-sour
and slightly crunchy. From bonobo also called
pygmy chimp by the fact that our young males
do not admit such lust they will fuck small trees
in public.

Indians: see CEMETERIES; also, GRAVES, MASS.

JPL is on the dry side of the dry side canyon that becomes Arroyo Seco
that becomes the Los Angeles River that becomes the water
that Mars supposedly had when Mars had oceans and one
phone is ringing right now in an empty beauty parlor
on the far side of Mars, there, can you hear it, I think
it is for you.

To have is to prove and to prove is to own, from Sadie Hawkins dates
to rare bird committees. The river checklists May's bent-billed
avocets, spreads a feast of brine flies for September sandpipers,
still counts on the presence of the killdeer whose high queer
scree scree calls reminded the first tidewater settlers of the
words in English, in the imperative voice, for each of them to
kill the deer, kill the deer. And so they shrugged and looked
across the turned-over earth and newly mown saltmarsh hay
and shouldered their Daniel Boone birdseye maple flintlocks
and did so, they killed the deer, ten or twenty times
a day.

What the river does not have are lapwings, jaunty Euro-plovers
wearing Robin Hood feather hats. Newfoundland does,
Maine maybe, but L.A. never had so much as one lapwing
shot and stuffed with corn meal (later cotton), tagged,
laid out in cutlery trays in a Foundation collection.
Probability pushstarts imagination up the hill:
in all the storms and years of history lost to us
like leaves shed from an immense and sad tree,
lapwings must have flown here at least once,
just a lost and rain-soaked once,
surely.

"Damn Mexicans. Ungodly outcast Romany spawn."
No Uncle. "Did you see that cat? They cut it,
cut right off the tail of that poor bushes cat.
Brownskinned ditch-fucking dirt eaters."
Please Uncle. "Cuntwad Mexicans." *Please sir,*
that is a Manx cat, it was born like that
from a baby kitten. It has no tail
because it came that way
from Jesus.

Nimbus in August, names' last chance: Frogtown, Avenues,
Toonerville, White Fence. Flaco is feeling up La Loca
behind Pioneer Chicken. She wears a new wifebeater
and two slaps of Romance by Ralph Lauren, hearts
outlined in eyeliner on the back of the novel
of her heart. And his hands are dark bottles
trying to shake out something, anything—
his hands are dark bottles and he knows
she is the one who can show him how
to hold his hands steady in the fire
until the glass softens and bends
then reassembles into a hundred
votive candles burning steady
in a small, dark,
holy place.

Oranges grew here, lemons, seed-rich persimmons. La Tuna,
a brushy pass named for cactus fruit. Manzanita,
little apple. Wild grape chokes wet canyons.
In Placerita gold was discovered in the roots
of an onion. To grow something, brochures

said, just scrape out two big fists of earth,
hold them up to the sky,
add some water, wait,
then pick the fruit.

Poly want a cracker, Poly want carnitas with extra guac?
Poly want to roost in honeysuckle and jacaranda,
kaffirboom coral or quince? Arcadia's feral parrots
commute to the fig groves of Cypress Park. Look,
there go seven cockatiels and a mitred parakeet.
Red-crowned parrots chase Rio Hondo's conures;
wheeling flocks of lilac-crowned parrots tease
the peacocks of Palos Verdes. Budgerigars
write daily postcards home: *Weather fine,*
so wish you were here.

Since Quetzalcoatl is sitting on the crossarm of a transmission tower
200 meters south of Fletcher Drive in moonlight calmly eating
a rusty-armored, twenty-to-thirty year old white male
head first, then he did leave Belize after the Conquest

alive after all, which means that we really do live
in the red lands of the east, and so—
well, okay then. Right on.

Rockets ride at high tide off of Long Beach, waiting for Bic lighters
of liquid oxygen to straddle the pontoons of the oil platform
launch ships towed into position at the Equator so that
XM Radio can lob a few hundred pounds of Bob Dylan
into near-earth orbit and what the deckhands say
is that it is really calm at sea and in a night launch
when the main chamber fires and lifts, it lights
up the ocean surface in a twenty-mile circle
like some kind of bioluminescent atomic
orchid.

Sugar. Sugar cane. Sure as sugar. Sugar Ray on the radio
when sugar baby tells you what he won't look
in your eyes to tell you. You're in Bette Davis
Picnic Area with no ride home leaning
on a tilted sycamore in the dying light

and here comes the sugar monster
to cut all of the bad sugar
out of your big fat heart.

The tundra swans grazing Ballona in 1910 were white needles
sewing their bills into the lowtide lawn. History
waited behind, like the man after church
waiting to sweep up.

Umbrella, fish tank, chemical burn—the night sky, humming.

Viridian smears: even if that is all algae is to us, a wiped rag
or a leaky spigot's leaky moss—and yes, this has circled
back to algae again and without the botanists this time—
even if that is all that it is, just what, exactly, have 9000
western sandpipers found to eat in the August slicks
of a smoggy concrete slab Vernon
afternoon?

Water in the ocean stands still and the waves move;
waves in the river stand still and water moves.
A man thinks that, at the breakwater, water shining
like pain. One way Mayans wrote *water* was to say
Reptile Eye, and another was, She of the Jade Shirt.
Think about that instead of the other things. Good.
Next pick a sample wave and time it, so that if (say)
peak to trough to breaking peak takes ten seconds, then
celerity = *g* (acceleration due to gravity) times T (duration),
divided by 2π=

$$\frac{980 \text{ cm/sec}^2 \text{ x } 10 \text{ sec}}{(2) \text{ x } (3.14 \text{ etc.})}$$

= 1,560 cm/sec or 15.6 m/sec or, roughly, 31 knots per hour
and so therefore, the ashes of the letter with her photograph
which you nudged from Hyperion Bridge yesterday should
pass the *Salicornia* of Long Beach and the red channel buoy
and through salinity's pycnocline and sink past the edge
of the circulation of your bad dreams in just over
five or six years.

X is the smallest no the biggest name of all
since as Christopher Smart said,
the names and numbers of the animals
are as the names and numbers
of the stars.

Yuma myotis eclipses western pipistrelle while a rare
Townsend's big-eared bat jitterbugs retrograde
to Venus. True, they shit while upside-down
and live under bridges like sad brown fruit
but can *you* catch a moth in your bare hands
in the dark, and do it again
in freefall, 600 times
an hour?

Zachery Ukiah was my best friend's step-grandfather's name
and when he picked us up after the *Planet of the Apes*
matinee we stopped to poke for frogs at the river
but the county bulldozers had just been there
and all the willows were scraped clean and

this man tall and bent like he had been hung
out wet from a clothesline in too hot of sun
and dried funny, just spit and said hell
I wouldn't skip a penny across water
this dirty, and we got in the car
and left.

The Flood of 1914

wrecked more than Hope
and Temple. That part

comes later. First is
storm drain love: it's

Valentine's Day so
I've painted a cat

for you—see, its ears
are red fire, the mouth

grins wide, one eye winks
at the blonde dolls' heads

watching from the back
of the grate. Plastic seals

the drain, soil builds, sedge
edges out rust-browned

mint. Call it modern
life, ecology's

99 cent store
riparian sublime.

Iron cats because
of a drunk uncle,

barracho El Niño.
Valentine week,

1914, it rained
nineteen inches

in three days after
two months of days

like that. The river
was a rushing sea,

a plumed spill, twenty
spewing flumes that

had to go somewhere
and so where they went

was Los Angeles.
Welcome to Long Beach

atoll. Ferries cross
San Fernando's lake;

Compton Creek spreads
half a mile wide. Lost,

a sideshow tiger
swam from Rio Hondo

to Orange County.
Arroyo Seco

spit houses like teeth.
A bridge rode to sea

with men still on it;
on Avalon Beach

they found dogs, cattle,
half a gabled roof.

Then came silt: harbor
sandbars rose so fast

cargo ships canted,
lifted high by mud,

miracle churches.
Let us bow and pray

for what to do next.
Blame the railroads

whose trestles made floods
worse; blame engineers

as false gods. Blame streets
for their slurried paving.

After blame comes bonds,
plans, piles, cement spans;

after blame comes *nature,*
you're not the boss of me.

Draglines and dredges,
the drudge years hauling

all the life away.
I've painted a cat

for you, see, its ears
look as if it listens,

at night, to voices;
maybe it hears

some lost person
back in 1914

insisting, *it didn't*
have to be this way.

Chiropterophily

Above – the face, shaped like a perfect heart.
Below – the heart's torn face.

—Ted Hughes, *Crow*

"**Clutter** can be thought of as just the distance to the nearest object from which a bat can pick up an echo. So a bat flying in the open, well above the ground and well away from any objects, may be in zero clutter, while a bat flying amongst tree trunks or along water close to a riverbank would be in high clutter. A bat emitting high frequency, low intensity calls may still be in low clutter even when flying just a few meters from objects, while a bat emitting loud, low frequency calls might be in high clutter even 30 meters above the ground. So the degree of clutter depends on the bat, as well as on the distance between the bat and something else."

—Chris Corben, from his website.

I am riding a bike
and thinking about clutter—

no, I am riding a bike
at dusk on December 1st
and thinking not about clutter
but about John Clare
("a blank notebook could cost him a week's wages")

I am riding a bike
along the river at dusk on December 1st
and thinking about my life's wrack and trill
when through the clutter of power lines I see a waterfall
of black starlight
disappear
into the slit
between oak gall and mouth gape, see
or think that I see a flick of the wrist assassin
slicing a wedge of midges free of the sedges
somewhere between the Baum bicycle bridge
and the edge rings of Venus—

I am riding my just-back-from-the-shop bike just at the head of winter
when I see a tiny ninja man jagged and dark flying on his hands

no

yes

it is the first day of December (*wrong date*) and I am riding alone
(*alone again*) afraid (*afraid again*) to say the D words aloud
(*Disneyland, Dinosaur, Dumbo Ride, Divorce*)
but is the first day of December
which is a winter month which means that is it too late
for summer flight and I stop my ride from Fletcher to self-pity
because there—no, *there*—

one late bat folds

creases in a post-windy, pre-smog Lucite-blue sky
that x-actos the twilight free of the palm trees
so cleanly that even my spokes

shine with the clarity of a slap
to the face
in a 1940s movie. *Thanks, I needed that—*

and I am off my bike now and trying to track it with binoculars
herky jerky flight, pale fur, tail in a membrane
like a leaf laminated in murky plastic,
yellow and black scalloped wings—

must be Hoary Bat, *Lasiurus* -something, and I am happy now,
I want to call somebody, I have my phone in my tool bag
and I think, hey, I am riding my bike and I have seen a bat
and who can I call, this is so cool, and then I think

what, are you fucked up? This is nature, you can't call somebody
when you're out in nature and I don't care if it is the middle of L.A.
and the freeway is running right by the river louder
than Grapevine Rapids in the Grand Canyon—

I mean (I say to myself) would John Clare
have reached for his cell phone when crossing the fens
he had heard some coffin creak twilight marsh sound,
called the vicar to explain that *Of the fox*
the stunted bark
                    is a sort of terror
coming from solitude deep
in the deeper solitude of night
which fear peoples with
peoples fears,
of robbers witches faireys & every other evil
but
(he would enumerate, continuing on with unlimited weekend minutes)
          worse the badger
whose yells are like those of a woman
under the
          agonys of murder
& in fact it is believed
his is

the noise of a spirit that has been murdered
& wanders
            dogging travellers
with its dismal cry.

He would not. A friend was leading a field trip once
at San Joaquin Marsh and standing on a willow stump
by a sea of cattails lecturing the assembled undergrads
when his phone went off in the middle of the talk
in the middle of the reserve and in one quick sweep
of his arm without breaking eye contact he reached down
and took it from his belt and flung it out into the sky
behind him and down into the eutrophic ciénega
forever—a splash like Basho's frog—and he kept
talking as thirty mouths gasped O and tried to understand
what this spontaneous act of terrorism
meant.

His story impressed me and I don't even like my phone,
can barely work it, could not,
                                        that day,

remember who it was I was supposed to call,
could not imagine throwing a phone away
like a wife, as simple as upgrading rental flats
or switching calling plans. Death is a bat
dancing on piano wires
of seizure, watch him
twitch. Maybe

this one is hoping to sublease a place in Ensenada for the winter,
maybe he will wait and move in under the Tropico Bridge,
1925, rebuilt as the Los Feliz Bridge with dorsal fin walls
after the floods of '38, maybe he will stop right here
and move into the space between my fat skin

and my cut heart. Stupid bat, asked Coyote
drunk in love with Cactus Wren,
what do you know about life?

Ah life, said Bat.
                              Plenty, plenty.
Life is all I know. The problem is that

for me life is as light as moth powder
on the tongue
but for you
Coyote
                    life is the fingertip
          on the other side of the airport glass.

Hurry, Coyote, your flight is boarding.
Hand me your belt and shoes—
you must go now

we shipped your next wife ahead first class,
pass through the wands and smoke

so you can catch up.

Casitas

Homeboy takes his Zeiss for a walk,
inventing lies, sifting lives. It curls
and teases, memory—blisters history,
batons the moon-eyed drunk. Trust it
less than hearts. Just walk. Scan the bank,
pretending you don't care if you can't say
from when to when you lived on Casitas.
What was that? We're all just transients,
even the song sparrows and the wrens.
Did I really once see a dead man by the
tracks? We ate bearclaws before church.
I want that hubcap to be the dim crown
of a doubloon. I want to eat a great lunch
at a little place nobody yet knows. No,
what I want is for this narrative to be grand
canyons of accusing description or at least
a grand piano for childhood's loss. It pulls
back, refusing, the horse that won't load.

Did we live on Larga or Gardena then?
My father took me riding one Sunday
in Arroyo Seco, knew a guy who knew
a guy, and I sat there chck-chicking at it
until dad said, *what the hell are you doing,*
stop that you moron. Christ, use both reins,
use your heels. I slumped, soft and wet.
Even death was something better then.

Blurs skeet from view; binoculars pivot.
Is it a Lincoln sparrow or a winter wren,
a penny or a pen? I fiddle with the focus.
Birdwatching is for fags. Mountain men
and vaqueros used to kill bears here. Hard
light fills a confluence that now only kills cats
in burlap bags. Walk cement's angle of repose
listening to water crumple against car hulls,
shrug, move on. A river can be accessorized
with pocket parks and bike paths, still be
a scar yard. A duck limps, missing a foot.

Hard to admit that you know but don't care
that people drink L.A. River's water
and it's all they have for dinner.
Were we ever children, pet stroking
and bike coasting? Turn and look back.
Sooner or later we all want a cat
killed. Be honest. Hurled goldfish
unfurl like tiny flags, "Buckets of Rain"
playing too loud. You wanted a pony,
maybe got a little brother that shits,
maybe got a black eye, maybe got
evicted again. I saw a kingsnake
bite a rat when I was eight. I ran
and ran. Next year a woman took off
her shirt, her bra. Brown breasts. It ran
down my leg. Empty Valentine's box
in love with an empty milk carton,
each blank heart is, even yours,
even hers. Next time try not to put
so much dirt in the mouth of your emotions

when you bury them. Enjoy this turn
before we take it away. The gulls will,
and after them, crows. A line of stones
pens pollywogs. Try to move them before
the sun's try pot rends the flensed facts
of their lives into hair oil, memory, semen,
bitter gall. Somebody will be along with
a vinegar wad to suck from a spear.
It will all be over soon enough.

We moved to Casitas then, 'little houses.'
To reinhabit childhood is just to imagine
that the yet-to-come days will be better
than the day the babysitter's cat littered
on Ricky Barton's bed, yellow bedspread
floral with black blood because nobody
had told you that vaginas made kittens.
You knew what the dad would do next.
It was his job. Burlap was more common
then, and the moms' moms would have

worn it to school if they had to, made
book bags, wouldn't have wasted it
on sad cats or rugs for dogs. Rags
lasted a long time. Moms smoked.

I am sure better things happened than this,
and worse. Shall I talk about the cute boy
who touched my penis? Matchbox cars
and Keds. What if the afterlife is just this,
only more so. I should have saved better.
Save a dime for Sunday church, save
Green Chip stamps. We give each day
its daily twine. Who can pee higher
over the dead turtle? A neighbor girl
died of something that made her skin
too thin. Cars hit dogs. Dads hit cars
and folded in half. Sex lap, welt dance,
cop spit—river as Las Vegas, river as a place
in between all the other places, *nada*-place
to cut Scouts or char glass or bb the pigeons'

eyes closed. And at the end of the week,
by the Los Feliz bridge, river as the place
to shoebox the dead as we wade through
the wad-fisted mud and the water stains
our t-shirts and Glendale's air-raid minarets
ah-woogah out their 1965 calls for the faithful
to attend the prayers for the restoration of *El Río*
de Nuestra Señora de los Angeles de la Porciúncula.

Will there be rivers in Heaven, water bugs,
red sliders? What horses we will ride then.
To remember childhood is to balance short
against long, Tomorrowland against hunter
green lawns. Childhood is the kindled bier
the poet wakes up on, trussed with red cord.
Strange birds circle overhead as on the pyre
reeking of kerosene the poet twists, trying
to light a book of matches with his toes.
Yesterday he dropped them all. This time
he will get it right and even the sulkiest slick

of eddied backwash will unfold in the blue silk
of flame, will take a walk with black smoke—
and maybe this time even the bones of water
will burn themselves clean.

The Price of Dogs

Thou shalt not bring the hire of a whore, or the price of a dog,
into the house of the Lord *thy God.*

—Deuteronomy 23:18

Water in the desert,
hoo-rah.

It is a miracle,
wine and loaves,
loaves and fish heads:

not Cana but a river
& not a river but a system:

open channels, 470 miles;
covered storm drains, 2,400 miles;
curbside openings, 98,000;
debris basins, 123; reservoirs, 3;

dams, 3; crib dams 87; check basins,
even more;
                bridges,
more than that.

Except not so much a system as a conduit,
a conduit for water to be shoved away,
get yer hands offa me—
                                the straight man
rejecting the drag queen.

Except not so much boas and has-beens
as the exoskeleton of a once-wet floodplain.
But not so much a floodplain as a flood,
        waiting to happen, again.
                                Not a flood but the threat of a flood
and not a threat, but a symphony. The duck and the duck hawk
each have a part. The Tillman Wastewater Treatment Plant conducts.

Was that a cuckoo? Japanese poets heard the cuckoo's autumn coo-cooing
                and thought of cold nights,

            exiled lovers,
                                    dead children.
We could too except cuckoos nest in river corridors
not conduits. The name sounds like a strain of flu: *Coccyzus americanus*
and this one's call was more staccato and hollow than Japan's cuckoo
so make of that what you may. Gone from Los Angeles County,
Yellow-billed Cuckoo only lives in checklists of extirpated ornitholgies
                                    and the dreams of a lonely Issei farmer, 1938,
as the winter fog settles in around his Atwater Village bungalow
                            bringing the smell of fennel and damp smoke,
            and, faintly, something being baked at Van de Kamp's.
The radishes are good this year. He gets mail from Okahama,
gives a little money to the Association for Orphans,
                                                      is terrible at origami.

Normandy two seven zero seven one: over on Casitas in a palm tree
white bungalo frame house the painter Don Bachardy is growing up,
noticing rivers of colors and not knowing yet what to do with them.
Not so much the river as the memory of a river, and not so much that
as noir movies and a boy from another planet playing *La Migra* on the guitar

while his girlfriend drinks Colt 45. Not music
but shaved heads and a thin brown dog. Not dogs but coyotes
and not coyotes but mountain lions, at night, following the pet food
from the Santa Monicas to the Verdugos. President Ford,
campaigning in Glendale, called them the *Vertigos*
and was not far wrong. Not vertigo but terror and not terror
but slimes of kelp backwashing upstream somewhere near Wilmington
and not Wilmington but miles of refineries at sunset looking like
a scale model of Kirkuk being readied for a remake of *Blade Runner.*
Not a river but a sequel to a river and a big production at that—
more water, at high flood, than the Mississippi at St. Louis
and not oil refineries but miles of ships at anchor, GNP bathtub,
IMF regatta. But not Marx and trade deficits, harmless nostalgia
when replica schooners dock next to a red fire boat, a green kayak,
and twenty thousand cubic feet of air conditioning ducts.
From Canoga Park to the harbor, 51 miles of river, waiting.
The volunteer crews coil hemp rope imported from Taipei.
Single White Schooner looking for a Sugar Daddy. Is it you?
The future can always be different. If you want something,
say so. Lost dog sign: Water looking for Compton Creek,

last seen in 1948. No tags, no collar. Compton Creek is looking
pretty good, all things considered, let's do lunch some day.
Not Compton but thinking you see somebody you know
then saying their name aloud, but you are wrong. Not wrong,
just mistaken. Not mistaken, just misguided. Well-intentioned
but misguided. William Mulholland said, there it is, it is yours,
take it. And so we did, we took it, not misguided so much
as obedient. Yet rivers can be rebuilt, the radishes replanted,
the muskrats seen again, in the dim Atwater dawn. Trees
are not impossible. Stickleback linger, waiting. It is the future,
there it is, it is yours,

take it.

Photograph by Charles Hood

About the Authors and the Artist

Peter Bowler is a Senior Lecturer in the Department of Ecology and Evolutionary Biology at the University of California, Irvine, where he has taught for 28 years. He took his BA at Bard and four years later received his doctorate in biological sciences from UC Irvine, after which he was a National Research Council Postdoctoral Fellow at the National Museums of Canada in Ottawa. At present Bowler directs the UCI Arboretum, is campus coordinator of UCI's Natural System Reserves, and is the Co-Director of the Minor in Global Sustainability. He has published well over one hundred papers on topics ranging from ecological restoration of coastal sage scrub to lichen ecology and taxonomy to endangered freshwater snails in the Middle Snake River. He grew up in Bliss, Idaho, on the Snake River, and still enjoys the Snake River's beauty and ecology, as well as rafting and fly-fishing. His research interests are diverse, encompassing habitat restoration, open space conservation, and mitigation as they relate to biodiversity loss, particularly in coastal sage scrub and wetlands; rare, threatened and endangered species, especially in wetland and sage scrub habitats; lotic and lentic freshwater ecology; the chemical ecology of lichens, particularly in the Ramalinaceae; and environmental ethics. This is his first appearance in a poetry book—and, he hopes, not his last.

Photograph by Bruce Bartrug

Bruce Bartrug studied ornithology at Louisiana State University under George Lowery and John O'Neill, but found that life had other plans for him. At present he is an artist and pharmacist in rural Maine. He spent three years in the Army during the Vietnam conflict and was fortunate not to see the bloody Mekong until a recent trip to Cambodia. Yet despite his time in the Army and his grounding in the sciences, he has always been an artist at heart. Highlights in a half-century of nature study range from sketching rock art in Namibia to a sighting of the now-extinct Bachman's warbler in the *cheniers* of Cameron Parrish, Louisiana.

A member of the Guild of Natural Science Illustrators and various neotropical ornithology organizations, Bruce Bartrug has paintings and drawings in collections in South Africa, Chile, Argentina, and Ecuador. In addition, his work has been reproduced in *El Hornero*, the journal of the *Asociacíon Ornitológica del Plata*, and in several publications of the *Unión de Ornitólogos de Chile*. Recently he had a watercolor of a *Ramphocelus* tanager accepted into the first-ever art exhibit by the American Ornithological Society. Besides private comissions and his work in *Río de Dios*, he also recently illustrated *Under the African Air*, a collection of prose and poetry from Fountain Mountain Press, and is at work on several other innovative collaborations.

Photograph by Charles Hood

Charles Hood's garage stores a kayak, two mountain bikes, sixteen different backpacks ("one from each company, and doubles from Black Diamond"), and a complete set of Red Hen Press titles. A graduate of UC Irvine, he has studied tribal poetry on a Fulbright in New Guinea, and also has been a dish washer, a factory worker, a cross-country ski instructor, and a nature guide. Including sightings along the L.A. River, his list of California bird species is in the low 500s. Perhaps it was too much *Mutual of Omaha's Wild Kingdom* while young, but other groups attract him as well; in India he once set a record for the array of wild canids ticked in one hour: dhole, Bengal fox, golden jackal, Indian wolf, and a loping pack of feral pariah dogs "mean as razor wire." His recent books include *Under the African Air* (Fountain Mountain Press, 2006) and *The Half-Life of Salt*, subtitled "Voices of the *Enola Gay*." This is his second collaboration with Bruce Bartrug. Hood claims that his poetics are simple, in that he agrees with Charles Wright when he says that all poets are Language Poets, and agrees as well with Language Poet Clark Coolidge, who asserts that "poetry is always using / words you don't know."